He'd taken a shortcut through the buckbrush and wild mahogany and receding snowdrifts, when the thunder of galloping hooves rose in the west. Longarm turned, his right hand automatically going to the walnut grip of his double-action .44.

He kept the Colt in its holster, however. The horsemen were fast approaching, the ground vibrating beneath Longarm's low-heeled cavalry boots. There were too many riders—five or six—to fight off with only his Colt and double derringer, and with no cover within diving distance.

"Well, who do we have here?" he muttered to himself as the riders skidded their sweaty mounts to a collective halt before him, spraying dust over his boots.

Their faces were covered with burlap sacks, spaces for the eyes and mouths cut out. All five were aiming old-model carbines at him.

Longarm couldn't believe his luck would have soured this bad, but the chill hopscotching his spine told him he was about to meet the Hawk Haughton Gang sooner than expected—and, most likely, his Maker.

TABOR EVANS

LONGARM

AND THE HOLY SMOKES GANG

JOVE BOOKS, NEW YORK

THE BERKLEY PUBLISHING GROUP
Published by the Penguin Group
Penguin Group (USA) Inc.
375 Hudson Street, New York, New York 10014, USA
Penguin Group (Canada), 90 Eglinton Avenue East, Suite 700, Toronto, Ontario M4P 2Y3, Canada
(a division of Pearson Penguin Canada Inc.)
Penguin Books Ltd., 80 Strand, London WC2R 0RL, England
Penguin Group Ireland, 25 St. Stephen's Green, Dublin 2, Ireland (a division of Penguin Books Ltd.)
Penguin Group (Australia), 250 Camberwell Road, Camberwell, Victoria 3124, Australia
(a division of Pearson Australia Group Pty. Ltd.)
Penguin Books India Pvt. Ltd., 11 Community Centre, Panchsheel Park, New Delhi—110 017, India
Penguin Group (NZ), 67 Apollo Drive, Mairangi Bay, Auckland 1310, New Zealand
(a division of Pearson New Zealand Ltd.)
Penguin Books (South Africa) (Pty.) Ltd., 24 Sturdee Avenue, Rosebank, Johannesburg 2196,
South Africa

Penguin Books Ltd., Registered Offices: 80 Strand, London WC2R 0RL, England

This is a work of fiction. Names, characters, places, and incidents either are the product of the author's imagination or are used fictitiously, and any resemblance to actual persons, living or dead, business establishments, events, or locales is entirely coincidental.

LONGARM AND THE HOLY SMOKES GANG

A Jove Book / published by arrangement with the author

PRINTING HISTORY
Jove edition / March 2007

Copyright © 2007 by The Berkley Publishing Group.

ISBN: 978-0-515-14265-5

JOVE®
Jove Books are published by The Berkley Publishing Group,
a division of Penguin Group (USA) Inc.,
375 Hudson Street, New York, New York 10014.
JOVE is a registered trademark of Penguin Group (USA) Inc.
The "J" design is a trademark belonging to Penguin Group (USA) Inc.

PRINTED IN THE UNITED STATES OF AMERICA

10 9 8 7 6 5 4 3 2 1

Chapter 1

When a clock began chiming a Brahms piano concerto in his ear, Deputy United States Marshal Custis Long, known as Longarm to friend and foe alike, opened his eyes to see a tender pink nipple bearing down on him like a single-bore peashooter.

The nipple moved, and so did the pillowy breast beneath his left cheek.

"Cust-isss," complained the girl he'd been sleeping on.

Longarm blinked and pushed up on his arms, watching the two porcelain-pale orbs roll away from him as he tried to recall in that foggy bog of first waking who in the hell they belonged to. Then he saw the lush raven hair and straight, aristocratic jawline in profile as Cynthia Larimer rested her head back against the cream silk pillowcase.

Christ. If he was going to do the mattress dance with the niece of Denver's founding father, General William H. Larimer himself, he should at the very least keep a good grasp of the lady's name.

Longarm rose onto his elbows, fumbled around with the brass and cherrywood clock until he got the infernal Brahms to stop torturing his brandy-tender brain plate, then sagged back to the fine, warm bedding—as fine a mat-

1

tress sack and trimmings as he'd ever slept in outside of the boudoir of a French actress he'd once saved from Barbary Coast owlhoots. And that was a long time ago. . . .

"Custis, you're not really going to get up at this dreadful hour, are you?" Cynthia groaned, entangling her legs with his as she slitted her eyes at a window on the other side of the bed. "It's not even really *morning* yet!"

"I reckon I can doze awhile." Longarm spooned his long, muscular body against Miss Larimer's, crooking his left arm beneath his pillow and snaking the other around the girl's delectable, naked orbs, soft and warm as fresh cow's milk against his forearm.

The girl gave a satisfied trill and settled deep into the sheets. "That's more like it."

Longarm smiled as he snuggled down against her. They lay drifting back into the dream world together once more, until the wail of a Burlington locomotive made its way from the Union Yards to the Larimer family's fancy granite digs on Sherman Avenue a half mile away.

Longarm's eyes suddenly snapped open. He flung the covers back and shot his naked body out of bed like a cannonball fired from a howitzer.

"Nope," he said, smacking his lips and glancing out the lace-curtained window to his right, where the golden morning light was washing over the stark brown prairie west of Denver. "No, ma'am. It's time to rise and shine. I'm due in at Billy Vail's office at eight."

"Last time, we lounged about till ten!"

"That was before I'd turned over my new leaf."

Her voice was muffled by the sheets she'd pulled over her head. "What new leaf?"

Longarm stumbled around the high-ceilinged, finely appointed room, gathering his clothes which he—or she, rather—had strewn from the oak door to the bed. Through the brandy washing back and forth from one battered brain lobe to the other, he remembered they'd taken a hack from the opera house on Larimer Street, then fairly run through

2

the vast, vacant house—her aunt and uncle and most of their staff having gone back to the old family home in Pennsylvania for a time—tearing at each other's clothes like preadolescent nymphomaniacs.

"What new leaf, Custis?" Cynthia repeated beneath the sheets.

Longarm dumped an armful of clothes on the bed. "The new leaf that's gonna start puttin' me in at Billy's office on time for a change. You see, I had a birthday of late, and I was thinkin' I should mark it somehow—you know, with a change in my life."

"You mean, like a resolution?"

"That's it—a resolution." He splashed water into the porcelain bowl atop the washstand for a whore's bath, and instantly set about scrubbing his face, neck, and ears. "And that resolution, I decided, was to become less of a thorn in Billy's side." The cold water stung his face, and he shook his head like a dog. "Billy, he ain't as young as he used to be, and with all the federal budget cuts, he keeps getting more and more work dumped on his desk. It ain't right, me always showin' up late for work when he's got so many other burrs under his blanket."

"If you stay, Custis, I'll make you an omelette. I learned last month in Paris how to make them the way the French do."

Longarm chuckled as he sponged his privates. Apparently, making omelettes wasn't the only thing she'd learned to do in the French fashion, and he had the chafed cock to prove it.

"Next time, my flower."

"It's only seven."

"It's a long walk from your digs to the Federal Building, and I have to stop for my shave at the barbershop."

"Spoilsport," she complained through a yawn.

Hearing the girl's rhythmic breathing in the large, canopied bed behind him, Longarm quickly dressed, then stood before Cynthia's full-length mirror, appraising the brown tweed suit, string tie, and fawn vest adorning his rangy, six-foot-four frame.

He donned his snuff-brown Stetson, tugging the flat brim down cavalry-style, and swept two fingers over his John L. Sullivan mustache. Over the years, his face had been so severely scorched by the sun and wind that, in the room's frail light, it looked like a slab of cherrywood resting beneath his hat.

When he'd stepped into his low-heeled army boots and positioned his double-action Colt Model T .44-40 high on his left hip, butt-forward, he glanced around the room, looking for something.

Finally, he stopped, scooped from the thick rug by the door his gold watch chain. One end of the chain was clipped to his Ingersoll watch, the other to a solid-brass twin-barrel .44 derringer. Checking the time, he dropped the watch in his left vest pocket, the popgun into the right, sauntered to the bed, and stooped over the long, sleeping mound of girl.

He pulled the sheets and blankets down, slid a lock of raven hair back from her face, and planted a gentle kiss on her warm, right cheek. She stirred luxuriously, stretching. "Are you sure I can't coerce you into staying?"

"A whole passel of Apaches armed with poison-tipped arrows couldn't convince me to stay."

She turned her face to him, cobalt-blue eyes framed by tussled raven wings, lips pooched in a pout. "But it's my last day in town and I won't be back for a long, long time. . . ."

Longarm kissed her lips. They were full and soft and moist. His loins stirred, and he winced as she wrapped her arms around his neck, putting more energy into the kiss. She sighed and cooed, pulling him closer.

Her delectable body was supple and warm, and carnal images from last night began winging like birds behind his eyes. His heart quickened. He suppressed his desire. The resolution. He reached up and pried her hands from behind his neck. "Absence makes the heart grow fonder."

"Cus-tisss," she complained, frowning as she sank back against the pillow.

"Till next time, Miss Cynthia." He planted a quick kiss on her forehead. "That was a fine, swell evening. It sure was." He drew the blankets over her head, then strode to the door, fishing one of his three-for-a-nickel cheroots from a pocket inside his jacket and congratulating himself on his willpower.

He hadn't known he had it in him. It just goes to show what a man can do once he steels his resolve. . . .

Longarm stuck the cigar between his teeth, opened the door, and started through it.

"Custis."

He stopped, hesitated, glanced over his left shoulder. "My resolve is stronger than—"

"Couldn't you stay just a *little* while longer?"

Cynthia had thrown her covers back to reveal every inch of her pale, curving scrumptiousness. Her conelike breasts, arrayed between two swirling curtains of jet-black hair, pointed straight at him. Her long, creamy legs angled down the sheets, turned to one side, knees together, one slender pink foot resting atop the other. Her triangular black love nest peeked out from the valley between her slender thighs—the well-turned thighs of a girl who spent as much time riding blooded Thoroughbreds as visiting European art museums.

Longarm's vision swam. The floor pitched beneath his boots. Sweat popped out on his blazing forehead.

Cynthia stuck a finger between her lips and frowned thoughtfully. "I think I'd like to do it doggy-style." Hair flying, she flipped onto her belly and rose up on her hands and knees. She looked at Longarm over her left shoulder, hair flowing off her right. "Like this!"

The view revealed to Longarm was not one he'd wish on his worst enemy, if said enemy had steeled himself against temptation, that is.

He gulped. "Listen, you're takin' unfair advantage."

As sweat trickled down his cheeks and his shaft drew

5

his trousers uncomfortably tight about his hips, he fished his Ingersoll from his vest pocket and flipped the lid.

"Oh, for chrissakes! You're takin' unfair advantage."

"Only because I can't bear the thought of not having your big stick in me one more time, Custis!"

"All right, Miss Cynthia." Longarm was already out of his boots and shrugging out of his jacket. "I've got time for one quick romp if I half-run and maybe catch a ride in a coal wagon headed for Colfax."

"You could just quit the nasty ole business of chasing unwashed outlaws altogether, and join me on my cultural excursions. You'd like Italy."

Longarm was only half-listening to the girl's timeworn monologue. He was staring at her round, pink rump, fairly salivating as he threw his shirt across the room and began peeling out of his balbriggans.

"Ever since Daddy died, I've had more money than I can ever spend in one lifetime. I see no reason why—*oh, God, Custis, careful with that thing!*"

Longarm had fairly leapt onto the bed and, hands grasping her hips, shaft fully engorged and extended, was working the lips of her snatch over the swollen head. As he inched into her, she yelled, "Oh God, oh God, oh *God*!"

Longarm drove his piston in and out of Cynthia Larimer while keeping an eye on the clock, and gauged his rhythm accordingly. She sighed, groaned, sighed, and groaned, throwing an occasional keening whine into the mix until she lifted her head up and threw her hair down her back.

"Ahhhhhhhhhhhhohhhhhhhhgawwwwdddd!

Her head and shoulders sagged forward, and she slumped to the pillow.

Longarm pulled out, leapt off the bed, gave his privates a cursory sponge, and ran around gathering his clothes once more.

Cynthia lay facedown on the bed, arms and legs spread, as though she'd fallen from a great height, breathing as though she'd run a great distance.

"Let's try this again, with less foolishness," he said, leaning over the bed as he buckled his pistol belt around his waist. He kissed the back of her head. "Good-bye, Miss Cynthia. Let me know when you're back in town."

He wheeled and jogged to the door.

"You'll be the first to know, Custis," she wheezed as he turned down the cavernous hall and drew the door closed behind him.

Longarm met up with no coal wagons heading in his direction, though plenty were rattling toward the brownstone mansions of the ranching and mining swells he'd just left. Still, having decided to forgo the trim and shave, he made good time, striding along the tree-lined cinder paths still damp from a recent spring rain, heading for the business flats near the confluence of Cherry Creek and the South Platte River.

The April morning air was crisp, and his breath puffed in the sparkling, high-altitude sunshine. Judging by his pocket watch, if he kept walking east at his current pace, he'd be mounting the Federal Building's broad stone steps at exactly five minutes of eight.

He was making such good time, in fact, that when he'd crossed Cherry Creek and was traversing a broad intersection choked with milk wagons and lumber drays, he slowed to a jog and grabbed an egg sandwich from a street vendor's bin. He tossed a coin to the scrawny lad in a straw boater and apron, and turned toward the U.S. Mint.

He hadn't taken two steps before a young man in a shabby bowler and glasses materialized from the recessed door of a bathhouse. Longarm stopped, nearly running the kid down.

"Y-you're Deputy U.S. Marshal Custis L-Long?" the stocky lad trilled, his dimpled jowls quivering, silver-rimmed spectacles flashing in the climbing morning sunlight. He held a newspaper like a prayer book in his right hand.

7

"Who wants to know, sonny?" Longarm said around the egg in his mouth, frowning with annoyance.

He had sixteen minutes, and it wouldn't hurt to be early.

"Swallow one for Disgusting Dan Dillon, you murderin' bastard!" the younker shouted, raising his newspaper toward Longarm, two inches of rusty gun barrel protruding from the end.

Chapter 2

This wasn't the first time someone had tried to clean Long-arm's clock, but it was arguably the first time it had been attempted so ineptly. The newspaper was a dead giveaway. The kid's nervously twitching face was another.

At an intersection near the Cherry Creek bridge, two blocks from the Federal Building, the younker was raising the gun. He'd just flung the newspaper away with his free hand, when Longarm stepped back and whipped his right leg straight up. His stovepipe cavalry boot connected soundly with the would-be assassin's wrist.

"Ahhk!" shrieked the kid as the old Navy Colt, which he hadn't even finished cocking yet, flew over his shoulder to clatter in the sandstone street behind him. He gritted his teeth and pinched his eyes behind his glasses as he clutched his wrist to his belly. "Son of a bitch!"

Longarm switched his egg sandwich to his left hand and grabbed his .44 with his right. "Who the hell you callin' names, you little privy snipe?"

The kid's eyes snapped wide at Longarm's revolver. Whimpering like a whipped dog, he turned and stumbled off down the sidewalk.

"Goddamnit!" Longarm barked. "Get back here, pip-squeak!"

Still clutching his hand before his waist and running as though he had a full load in his drawers, the kid passed a millinery shop and continued toward a lumberyard.

Reluctantly, hearing precious seconds tick off the pocket watch in his head, Longarm shoved his sandwich in his jacket and ran after the snipe. This little diversion was sure to make him late to Chief Vail's office, but he'd be damned if he was going to let the little bushwhacker get away scot-free to practice up for another try.

Fifty feet from the lumberyard, Longarm stopped and extended the Colt in his right hand. "Stop there or take one in the ass!"

As he ran, the kid lowered his head and dipped his right hand in his coat pocket. Pulling the hand out of the pocket, he stopped in the middle of the intersection and wheeled toward Longarm. "You killed my brother, Disgusting Dan Dillon," the kid spat, tears streaking his pudgy cheeks as he raised a single-bore peashooter. "Shot him and threw him in a privy. Our ma sent me to avenge my brother, and I aim—"

The roar of a wagon sounded on the far side of the lumberyard. The ground shook beneath Longarm's boots. The kid turned left. His lower jaw sagged.

An Irish-accented voice roared above the wagon's din, "Haul ass, fool!"

But the kid didn't have time to take a step, much less evacuate the intersection. The wagon shot out from behind the lumberyard's main building like a locomotive on a downgrade.

The kid screamed as the mule closest to Longarm laid the kid flat with his right shoulder. The kid bounced and rolled, caught up in the harness rigging. As the wagon thundered through the intersection, the kid disappeared under the box.

"Whooo-ahhhhh!" the driver bellowed.

The wagon stopped before a tobacco shop, the driver

cursing as he set the brake and wrapped the reins around the brake handle. The dog who'd been sitting in the seat beside the driver—a wiry, spotted mutt—leapt down and began sniffing the ground. The driver met Longarm off the wagon's right rear wheel.

"What in tarnation was that fool kid doin'?" the driver yelled. "Didn't he hear me comin'?"

Longarm pinched his trouser legs up his thighs and peered beneath the wagon. He winced at the grisly scene— he hadn't seen a body broken in such horrific fashion in a long time—and ran a hand along his jaw as he straightened. "I reckon he had other things on his mind, not the least of which was perforatin' my hide."

"He was trying to kill you, Longarm?" Most of everyone in this section of town—at least those who frequented the deputy's primary watering holes, as this man did— knew Longarm by his more familiar handle.

He didn't answer the driver. His gaze was cast two blocks up street, where a beat cop was heading this way at a fast pace. Longarm recognized the posture of Sergeant Bjorn Stanley. He turned to the Irishman, who was trying to coax his dog out from under the wagon, where it was giving the dead kid a thorough sniffing.

"Do me a favor, will you?" Longarm said, consulting his pocket watch once more and noticing he still had three minutes to get to Chief Billy's Vail office. The attempted assassination was nothing more than an annoyance to a man who had to parry similar assaults at least once every three weeks. "Give ole Stanley the lowdown on what happened here. Tell him I'll file a report with the coroner's office soon as I can. There'll be a drink in it for you over to the Black Cat later."

"All right, all right," the Irishman groused, reaching under the wagon for his dog, his big face red with exertion. "But this better not take too long, 'cause I gotta a timetable to keep my ownself!"

Longarm threw an arm up in acknowledgment and, taking another bite out of his sandwich, headed for Colfax one block west. He was too damn close to Billy's office to give up now. Who knows when he'd be able to manage such a feat again?

Strolling past the U.S. Mint, tipping his hat at the tweed-clad clerks and uniformed guards milling on the front steps, he checked his watch. Two minutes. Quickening his pace toward the Federal Building's imposing south entrance, he absently ran Disgusting Dan Dillon through the long list in his brain, and a couple synapses fired up a face to go with the handle.

Disgusting Dan was the hombre who'd tried to drill Longarm from the privy behind his boardinghouse on the other side of Cherry Creek, about two years back. Apparently, he hadn't been happy about the half-dozen years he'd spent in Yuma Prison after Longarm had tracked him down for stealing Indian beef and performing obscene acts upon a Pima squaw, and threw the shackles on him. The night of the attempted ambush, Longarm had punched a handful of .44 slugs through the privy door and into Disgusting Dan's belly. Disgusting Dan had fallen through the shithouse bench and into the very shit itself.

He'd blown up a few bubbles, and drowned. . . .

An appropriately disgusting end for Disgusting Dan. Obviously, his old lady had taken enough umbrage to ram another knuckleheaded nestling into the breech. Longarm wondered how many disgusting sons Mrs. Dillon had in her loading tube. . . .

"Mornin', Henry!" Longarm stepped through the oak door on which the words U.S. MARSHAL WILLIAM VAIL were stenciled in gold-leaf lettering, and tossed his hat on the rack.

The pimple-faced clerk pounding a sandwich of onionskins and carbon paper with his typewriter keys kept his nearsighted eyes on the newfangled machine, and continued pecking away with the practiced ease of a true paper pusher.

12

"Go right in. Marshal Vail has been waiting for you, Deputy Long."

"Waitin' for me, bullshit," Longarm grumbled, striding to Vail's door flanking the boy's desk. "I'm likely to give him a heart stroke, comin' in a whole fifteen seconds early."

"You might wipe the crumbs from your beard stubble," Henry advised with a desultory air, fingers flying over the keys.

Longarm scowled at the clerk, then brushed at his bristled cheeks and mustache. Bread crumbs and dried egg rolled down his chin and bounced off his vest to the tiled floor. "You sure got good peripheral vision for a four-eyes."

He stepped into Vail's office, drew the door closed behind him, and looked down at the pudgy, balding chief marshal hunkered over the papers on his blotter. Longarm was grinning so wide his face hurt.

"Mornin', Chief!"

Without looking up, but penciling a note on a yellow pad, Vail said, " 'Bout time you showed up. I don't have all morning, for crying out loud, Longarm. Sit down!"

"But, Chief . . ."

"I don't have time for your foolishness either. We've got important business here. Very important, and very *dangerous*. I've been pondering it since late yesterday afternoon, when I first got the wire from Lulu City."

Longarm raised an arm to the banjo clock on the oak-paneled wall. "But Billy, just take a look—"

Vail shook his head and sat back in his swivel chair. He took a deep puff from the fat stogie in his fist and fingered the sole remaining hair strand on his pink pate as if reassuring himself it was still there. "I'm gonna have to send you out on a bad one. One that could involve a whole passel of hardcases. And when I say passel, I mean they probably outnumber you twenty to one."

With a sigh and one more parting glance at the banjo clock, Longarm sank into the red Moroccan leather chair

13

angled before the chief marshal's mahogany desk. "Well, I've been outnumbered before, plenty of times, Chief."

"Not like this. You ever heard of the Hawk Haughton Bunch?"

Longarm frowned as he dug a cheroot from his shirt pocket. "Don't recollect the name."

"Hawk Haughton and his brothers, Ephraim and Lewis, used to wreak all kinds of havoc in Texas and south of the border in the years right after the war. They were all sent to the federal lockup by some of my old comrades in the Texas Rangers a few years back, for raiding army supply trains, organizing their own militia with the intent of overthrowing the U.S. government, and several other sundry transgressions which Uncle Sam found not only impolite but downright unpatriotic. Scalp-hunting on reservations and rape of several army officers' wives they found in a sacked wagon train not least among them."

"How in the hell did they end up free? Weren't they cold-stored for life?"

"I'm gettin' to that, and don't throw that lucifer on the floor." Billy Vail scowled at the spent match smoking between Longarm's right index finger and thumb, and slid his ashtray forward. "We civilized folk use *ashtrays*."

Longarm, about to toss the match to the threadbare rug, leaned forward and dropped it in the ashtray.

"By the time you're old enough to retire, I might finally have you potty-trained," Vail said, his chair squawking as he leaned back behind his smoke cloud. "The Hawk Haughton Bunch broke prison when they were being moved to another facility in Fort Worth, where they were supposed to be hanged. Members from their gang apparently hoofed it up from Mexico, shot a handful of guards, sprang Hawk and Ephraim—one of the guards sent Lewis to his Maker with a bullet through his left eye—and hightailed it back down to Mexico."

Billy puffed his stogie and tossed a manila folder at Longarm. "That was eighteen months ago. Sometime after that, they moved into the Rockies and began preying on ore trains—namely the narrow-gauge rig that ships smelted gold bars from the Holy Smokes Mine in Lulu City to Colorado Springs, where it's transferred to the Burlington line headed for Denver. Lately, however, it hasn't been making it to Colorado Springs, much less Denver. It's been hit a total of five times in the past year. Last time it was hit, two sheriff's deputies, two guards hired by the mine, and a fireman were killed."

Longarm riffled through the manila folder a half-inch thick with wanted fliers of owlhoots suspected of riding with Hawk Haughton—ex-Confederate soldiers, to a man. If they were all guilty of what they were being charged with—bank and train robbing, kidnapping, murder, and rape—it would be a pleasure to hunt them down. "I reckon the lawmen endin' up dead is why it's under federal jurisdiction?"

"That and the fact that the gold's being shipped to the U.S. Mint, to be turned into currency."

"You want me to head up thataway, see what's what and who's who, and arrest the thievin' bastards."

"No."

Billy leaned forward and rested his elbows on his paper-littered blotter. Deep lines cut into the bridge of his broad, pale nose.

"I want you to go up there, see if this really is the Hawk Haughton Gang—locally, they're called the Holy Smokes Gang now, for the mine they're about to run out of business—and see where they're holin' up. They're slippery as banana slugs. Might be hunkered down in a cave or an old trapper's shack in the high country. The sheriff and several seasoned trackers haven't been able to follow their trail."

"Why do they think it's Hawk Haughton's gang, Billy?"

"'Cause he—or at least someone who looks a hell of a lot like him—and his brother Ephraim have been seen in Lulu City and other mining camps in the same area. He's one brash son of a bitch, that Haughton. A cold-blooded killer."

Vail poked a stubby finger across his desk, slitting one eye. "Anyway, you are not under any circumstances gonna try to arrest the entire gang your ownself—do I make myself clear, Custis?"

Longarm smiled. "Billy, are you worried about me?"

"I'd send more men right now if I had 'em, but that counterfeiting racket over east and the postal thievery down south, not to mention the rigged voting up Dakota way, has got me stretched so thin I might have to place Henry on guard duty in the federal courts upstairs."

"He'd shoot his foot off."

"As soon as you figure out where the hardcases are holed up, I'll send cavalry from the Silver Bow outpost. I'd send 'em sooner, but nothin' like cavalry blues to send owl-hoots bustin' ass for Mexico."

"I prefer workin' solo anyways." Longarm had worked with other lawmen before, but found that even the best ones cramped his often unorthodox style.

"This is one job where workin' solo's liable to get you shot or worse and dumped into a ravine where only the mountain lions can find you. Hawk Haughton's boys are no doubt stealin' all this gold to finance another run at rebellion. That's how fuckin' crazy they are. And determined. They won't think nothin' about greasing a lone federal lawman nosin' around the rocks and snowdrifts up there, so don't get cocky!"

"Far be it from me." Longarm closed the folder. "Can I take this?"

"It's yours."

"No doubt a three-day trip from here. When do I leave?"

"The flier leaves for Colorado Springs at noon. There, you'll hop the narrow-gauge to Lulu City. Henry's typing up the expense vouchers for you now. Your rail tickets are on his desk. Keep track of your expenses and remember, Custis, the reform administration of President Rutherford B. Hayes will not pay for your cigars, rye, or sporting girls."

16

Longarm stood as he stuffed the manila folder in an inside jacket pocket, and snorted. "I've never paid for it in my life, Billy!"

"Speaking of women," Vail said as a reluctant afterthought. "You won't be traveling alone."

Longarm scowled. "Say again?"

"The daughter of the gent who runs the Holy Smokes Mine. She's passin' through Denver on her way to Lulu City. Been to some teachers college back East somewhere, but she's finished for the summer. Her pap, the mine owner, Solomon T. Gandy, has requested that the lawmen I send to investigate the robberies—a man, he hopes, of the 'utmost integrity and professionality'—accompany her home. Since I don't currently have a man with those qualifications at my disposal, you'll have to do, Custis, and you can wipe that grin off your face right now."

"Just a gas pang from my breakfast sandwich, Chief." A pretty traveling companion might lend color to an otherwise dull train ride, but with the way Longarm's luck was running, his charge would probably turn out to be both whiny and ugly.

"Now, while we don't normally hire out as bodyguards, I told the gent you'd do it . . . since by pure coincidence you and Miss Gandy will be riding the same train and all, and in light of the gang of cutthroats on the prod up there."

"Are they hitting the trains headed up *toward* the mine too?"

"Of course not. There'd be no reason to, since they aren't carrying anything more valuable than coal and a handful of passengers—mostly miners. But Miss Gandy's traveling alone, and you know how fathers are when it comes daughters."

Longarm chewed his cigar. "Not from personal experience."

"Fatherhood might even happen to you someday, Custis. When you finally get tired of chasing tail, decide to grow up, or"—Billy smiled crookedly and winked—"fall in love."

The thought of responsibilities beyond his job made Longarm's innards lurch. Day by day, he'd seen what similar obligations had done to Billy himself, stuck behind a desk while his pate balded, his middle widened, and his eyes turned dull with boredom. Longarm might die alone in some rocky desert or remote canyon, but by God, he'd go out with a flat belly and his pistol empty.

"Praise be to God, Chief!"

Vail shook his head and snorted ruefully. "Anyway, you're to meet Miss Gandy at the train station, under the big clock, at eleven forty-five." Billy spread his pudgy hands. "And let me stress that you and she, Custis, will be riding the train and *not* each other!"

"Billy, I'm offended!"

"Cut it out. Now, I've never seen this girl before. Henry has her description written out with your train ticket. But I don't care if she's better lookin' than this Miss Sarah Bernhardt you're so almighty fond of—if you trifle with this girl, Custis, I will have you beheaded and skinned alive, *and I will use your hide to reupholster that chair you're sittin' in!*"

Longarm chuckled without mirth. Some days, no matter how hard you tried to please, you ended up at a whipping post with your ass bared. He might as well have taken his time with Miss Larimer and enjoyed that post-coital omelette she'd offered. "Billy, you actually think I'd take advantage of some would-be schoolmarm who's fallen under the umbrella of my professional services?"

"I think you'd fuck a ham sandwich if it smiled at you pretty. Don't forget her pappy's name. Solomon T. Gandy. One Ebeneezer Coleridge, the superintendent, is your contact man at the mine."

"Gandy and Coleridge—I got 'em," Longarm grumbled as he headed for the door. First, his punctuality isn't appreciated, and then he's treated like a back-alley mutt.

"And Longarm," Billie called as the deputy opened the office door. "While you're waitin' on that train, get yourself a shave and a haircut. You might consider a new pair of trousers and a boot shine as well. And *last but not least,* I don't think the president's wife, Miss 'Lemonade Lucy' Hayes, would approve of a federal lawman coming to work with the aroma of sex on his person." Billy took a long pull from his stogie, glowering eyes slitted. "Have yourself a real bath for a change."

Longarm sighed, a whipped schoolboy facing his master. "Billy, did you even notice I was early this morning . . . even after some privy snipe tried turnin' me *toe-down*?"

Vail glanced at the banjo clock and blinked with mock surprise. "You were? No shit? Try making a habit of it, and get the hell out of here!"

Longarm slouched through the door and closed it behind him. Henry was scratching a pen across a pay voucher, his pale cheeks flushed. As Longarm moseyed to the outside door, Henry tried to cover a chuckle by loudly rolling fresh paper and carbons into his typewriter.

"I heard that."

Henry said primly as he began typing again, "Your dossier will be ready in an hour, Deputy Long."

Longarm stepped through the door. As he pulled it closed, he said without looking over his shoulder, "Kiss my ass, Henry."

Chapter 3

Longarm's first order of business after leaving the Federal Building was to head for the police station. There, over a couple of shots of Maryland rye with his old friend Sergeant Nat Delaney and the coroner, Howard Sharpton, he took care of the paperwork concerning the little snipe who'd tried to grease him with an out-of-date Civil War pistol.

Zackariah Dillon had been the kid's name, printed on a train ticket tucked away in his coat pocket. According to the date on the ticket, the lad would have been heading home to Raton on the very train Longarm was hopping for Colorado Springs. Longarm had half a mind to use the kid's ticket himself, to deliver the news of the younker's demise to his mother. But then, he didn't have any solid evidence she'd put the lad up to it, other than the lad's own words, that is, and why waste time on the old bat anyway? Chances are that, unless she was crazier than a tree full of owls, when the coppers informed her that young Zackariah had hopped a cloud for the Great Hereafter, she'd turn her horns in—or at least decide against sending any more sons to the boneyard.

Even after he'd prissed himself up with a bath, a shave,

and a haircut—his clothes were just fine as he probably wouldn't be seeing President Hayes's persnickety wife anytime soon—Longarm had a couple of hours to kill. So he picked up his traveling papers at the Federal Building, then took a meandering stroll, enjoying the spring sunshine and the girls in their light spring frocks, to his furnished digs on the other side of the Cherry Creek bridge. He retrieved his Winchester, war bag, bottle of Maryland rye, and sheepskin coat—it was still winter in the mountains around Lulu City—then informed his landlady he'd be gone for a few days.

At the Black Cat on Larimer Street, over a couple of beers and a venison sausage sandwich, he stripped, cleaned, and reloaded his Winchester, derringer, and Colt .44. When he'd popped the last pill into the Colt's wheel, leaving an empty cylinder under the hammer, he polished off his second schooner, then moseyed over to the Union Depot to meet the Burlington flier and his female charge.

Miss Gandy wasn't hard to pick out. As prearranged, she was sitting under the huge clock on the north wall, and she couldn't have looked more like a would-be schoolmarm if she'd been holding a thick wedge of chalk in one hand, a ruler in the other.

She was one of those girls, plain-featured to begin with, who seemed to actually try to make themselves look frumpish. This girl was doing a good job of it in her spruce-green traveling dress, adorned with only a few lengths of scalloped lace down the front, and a straw boater around which a wide strip of brown ribbon was tied. If she had breasts, her corset had drawn them flat to her chest.

Her brown hair was mostly hidden by the hat, with no pretty little curlicues that more fashionable girls arranged about their ears and cheeks. Miss Gandy sat with a book in her lap, her pale face tipped to read, knees together, her low-heeled, black-patent shoes primly curled together beneath the varnished oak bench.

Standing over the girl, Longarm said her name. She

21

looked up, brown eyes crinkling at the corners, as if annoyed at having been disturbed—a plain, delicate face neither pretty nor ugly, but somewhere in between. "Yes?"

"I'm Deputy Long—your, uh, escort."

She glanced at the clock behind her. "It's about time, Mr. Long. I was beginning to fear we'd miss the flier."

Longarm glanced at the clock then too. He was only two minutes late, and if the flier ever pulled out of the station on time, he'd know that hell had frozen over and the devil was sporting icicles in his beard. No point in starting out on the wrong foot, however, so he held his tongue.

He gestured at the long, telescoping carpetbag beside her, upon which rested a small, plain reticule. "Is that your only luggage, miss?"

"Certainly. I don't believe in burdening myself and others with a ton of unnecessary garments and goo-gaws I couldn't possibly wear in a month of Sundays, like *some* women."

Miss Gandy cast a disapproving glance at a middle-aged belle sitting on a bench behind Longarm, reading a newspaper. A plump, rosy-cheeked blonde, the woman was dressed in a frilly silk gown and enormous picture hat sporting flowers and berries that wouldn't be anywhere near ripe this time of the year. Luggage of all sizes and styles was stacked around her like a bunker against an infantry charge.

Reaching for the leather handles of the girl's bag, Longarm chuckled. "My back appreciates your good sense."

"Shall we then?" The girl slipped a marker into the fat hardcover book she'd been reading—something by a Henry James—then stood and grabbed her reticule. "I'd hate to miss the train."

"As would I, miss."

She glanced at him appraisingly, then turned and started toward the doors and the platform beyond. As she strode, taking quick, haughty steps, she regarded him over her left shoulder, the front of her hat rising and falling quickly as she gave Longarm another quick up-and-down. "You're tall, aren't you?"

"Tall to short folks, short to tall folks."

"Are you college-educated?"

"No, ma'am," Longarm said dully, threading his way through the crowd milling about the platform and the coach cars pulled up before the depot. "I can read street signs, though, and cipher numbers up to a hundred, though I do have to use my fingers and I'm often obliged to remove my boots in order to tally my bar bill."

She glanced back at him again, her eyes wide with surprise and appreciation. "A man of wit!"

"Sometimes, ma'am," Longarm said, following the girl up through the narrow entrance of a coach car, "wit is all us unschooled folks have against the educated classes."

The girl stopped as they left the vestibule and entered a car being flooded by travelers from the other end. People from this end were shoving past Longarm and Miss Gandy, scurrying to vacant seats on either side of the narrow aisle. The air smelled of sweat, tobacco, and coal smoke.

Looking around at the shabby car with its sooty bracket lamps and crudely upholstered bench seats, Miss Gandy made a wretched face. "Father usually buys me first-class tickets, so I'm accustomed to traveling in sleeper compartments."

"What happened this time?" said Longarm, sidling against her as a hefty woman with a thick Russian accent squeezed past them, dragging a small boy in a shabby bowler and threadbare topcoat.

"The Pullmans were all booked."

"Perhaps it'll be good for your humility to mingle with us commoners," Longarm drawled, taking the girl's arm and ushering her down the aisle.

He chose a seat about halfway down and on the car's right side, so he could watch the sun angling over the Front Range in the west. He wished the girl's father had been able to book her a sleeper, for she'd have been out of his hair that way.

He'd been in her company for less than fifteen minutes, and her snotty airs were already starting to chafe. It wouldn't have been so bad had she been prettier, but having to parry the insolence of a mousy little thing such as Miss Gandy, with her nasal voice and pinched-up face, was a tough pill to swallow.

As he tossed her bag onto the overhead rack, he was comforted by the prospect of trips to the smoker car for rye and cigars. He might even be able to rustle up a poker game, as he'd seen a dozen or so drummers lounging about the depot house earlier.

Visits to the smoker car probably didn't fall under the definition of "escorting," but he hadn't been given specific instructions as to how much time he had to actually spend at Miss Gandy's side. He'd check on her from time to time, but since she was neither sunny nor comely, he doubted anyone would trifle with her.

Longarm let her choose her seat, and when she'd settled down beside the window, he slumped into the aisle seat to her left. She blew her nose into a pink handkerchief, then tucked the handkerchief into her left dress sleeve, leaving a little triangle peeking out, and opened her book. She sniffed, licked her upper lip, and promptly began reading.

As her head lowered and her eyes slitted, two little persnickety lines of concentration etched the bridge of her nose, warding off interruptions.

Longarm didn't want to talk to her either. He'd no doubt get tired of picking thorns from his pride.

When all the passengers had settled into their seats, and the train lurched and chuffed southward out of the Union Depot yard, coal smoke and glowing cinders wisping around the windows, Longarm yawned, scratched his head, and considered the prospect of a cigar in the smoker car.

He only had five cigars for three days of travel, however. Better to conserve. Besides, he should endure the first hour of travel here with Miss Gandy. She already had him pegged as one of the lower classes, and Billy Vail was big on public relations.

That decided, Longarm hiked a cavalry boot on a knee and opened the *Rocky Mountain News* he'd purchased earlier. But just when he'd started to read, Miss Gandy lowered her book suddenly, scooted up slightly to look over the front and back seats, then leveled an enervated gaze at him.

She whispered, "Do you think this train will be robbed, Deputy Long?"

Longarm frowned. "Why do you ask, Miss Gandy?"

She bit her lip and shuttled her gaze around the swaying, creaking car. "I'm always . . . you know . . . hearing about train robberies out here. And reading about desperado gangs in the papers. There's one gang in particular that seems especially savage and ruthless. Just as bad as ex-Confederates. What are they called?"

She swung her eyes to Longarm, and raised her voice above the clacks of the wheels hammering over the rail seams. "Oh, yes. The Finn Bunch. They're supposed to be worse than that Jesse James and his depraved cousin, Cole Younger. The Finn Gang not only steals money from the passengers, but they do unspeakably craven things to the women."

She shuddered and crossed her arms on her chest. As she did so, her book slipped out of her fingers and tumbled to her lap. As it rolled off her lap, pages fell out of it, and the whole works landed on the scarred wood floor at her feet.

"I'll get it!" Miss Gandy cried.

Longarm had already reached for it. Arm extended, he froze.

There were two books on the floor. One was the fat tome by Mr. James. The other was a slimmer, yellow-covered book bearing the title *Ugly Jim Finn's Railroad Desperadoes* and a painted drawing of a train below the evil-eyed face of a black-hatted cutthroat, a green neckerchief concealing his nose and mouth, a blazing six-gun in his hand.

25

A corner of Longarm's mouth rose as he gathered the two books. "Here's your book by that James fella, Miss Gandy, and there's the one by Mr. Dead-Eye Dick." He emphasized Dick.

She grabbed both books out of Longarm's hands, her cheeks flushed, eyes downcast. "Thank you. I was using the penny dreadful as a bookmark. I bought it for Father. He's always loved a good, fantastic yarn. The more outlandish the better . . . as long as the Devil gets his due, of course. Father's right pious."

"Now, about those train robbers," Longarm said, "not to worry. Ugly Jim Finn don't operate in these parts."

"I wasn't talking about Jim Finn, Deputy Long. Didn't you spy those three armed men in the waiting room back at the Union Depot?"

"Three armed men?"

"Yes, the unshaven ones with six-shooters and Winchesters. One even had a knife protruding from his boot well." She stared at Longarm, then bunched her lips and narrowed her eyes. "I know what you're thinking, but I've far too good a head on my shoulders to be influenced by anything as fantastic as the novels of Mr. Dead-Eye Dick."

"Miss Gandy," Longarm said, plucking a cigar from his shirt pocket, "most of the men on this train are no doubt armed. It is the frontier, after all."

"The men to whom I refer had a definite seedy look. Their guns, I could tell, were freshly oiled. As were their holsters. Would men oil their guns and holsters for a simple train ride?"

"I saw the three men you're talking about. They looked like ranch hands to me. And ranch hands—as you probably won't read about in the novels of Dead-Eye Dick— habitually take good care of their weapons because, one, they don't have much else to do when they aren't gathering cattle except to obsess about their accoutrements, and two, they never know when they'll have to rely on a revolver or

26

long gun to defend themselves against rustlers, rattlesnakes, crooked gamblers, or hungry mountain lions."

Miss Gandy blinked slowly and, chin raised haughtily, sagged back in her seat. "I just think you should keep an eye on them, that's all."

"I'm federal." Longarm bit off the end of his cigar. "Train robbery would be a territorial matter. Now, if you'll excuse me, I'm going to make my way to the smoking car."

She grabbed his arm. "Oh, please don't leave! Please don't leave! If you can read and not just look at pictures, I'll lend you a book. I have extras in my carpetbag. Would you be interested in the Etruscans perchance?"

Longarm stared over at the girl, one shaggy brown eyebrow arched, cigar drooping from his mouth. He was beginning to understand why she needed an escort. Without one, she was liable to harm herself if no one else, or get herself pistol-whipped by a gent less tolerant than Longarm, and thrown from the train.

"That's right kind of you." He eased back in his seat, rolled the cigar to the other side of his mouth, and snapped his *Rocky Mountain News* open on his lap. "I'll just look at the pictures in my newspaper here."

That seemed to settle her down. She gradually relaxed and opened her book. Or books. He wasn't certain which one she was reading, but he hoped it was the one by the James fellow. A girl with her overwrought imagination didn't need to be devouring the penny dreadfuls, which Longarm suspected she'd been doing at that teachers college, probably by candlelight after curfew.

Longarm read a good half the newspaper before his eyelids grew heavy. He let his head sag back against the seat, then tipped his hat brim low, and closed his eyes.

He didn't know how much time had passed before the shrill screech of brakes woke him suddenly, and he opened his eyes to find himself being thrown forward against the seat back directly ahead. Miss Gandy gave a small, clipped scream as she too flew forward, losing her books as well as her hat.

The screech of the brakes rose in pitch until Longarm winced against the pain in his ears and looked out the window over the girl's brown hair to see the dun prairie lurch to a halt. A herd of antelope in the middle distance had stopped grazing to turn and stare at the train, stiff-necked.

"Oh, my God!" cried Miss Gandy above the din of the other indignant passengers. "It's a holdup, isn't it?"

"Ah, shit," Longarm grouched, grabbing his own hat from the aisle. "It ain't a holdup. There's probably just some cows on the tracks. Happens all the time."

Longarm had just stood to help the big Russian woman, who'd tumbled into the aisle, when the forward door opened and boots pounded the car's wooden floor. The man who'd just entered was one of the three well-armed waddies from the Union Depot's waiting room.

Well, shit. Maybe he wasn't a waddie after all. If he were a waddie, there'd have been no good reason to be carrying that big rifle in both hands and to be ramming a shell into the breech.

"All right, everybody sit still and you won't get hurt," the "waddie" bellowed around the fat stogie in his teeth, aiming the rifle straight out from his shoulder. "This here's a *holdup*!"

Chapter 4

Longarm heard a gasp to his right. He raked his gaze from the desperado at the front of the coach to Miss Gandy half-sitting and staring straight ahead, her lower jaw hanging, her complexion pale as death.

"I told you, I told you," she muttered. "It's Ugly Jim Finn!"

At the front of the train, the desperado stared down his rifle barrel and shouted, "Everybody, sit down and shut up! Get your valuables out, and don't be holdin' out on me! Any of you men decide to go for your guns, please do. My day ain't complete till I've blown a hole in somebody's hide!"

He laughed evilly as he lowered the rifle, aiming it straight out from his right hip, then fished a burlap feed sack from his coat pocket. He snapped out the sack, and holding the sack by the lip, began moving down the aisle. "Come on, come on. Get out those wallets and coin purses and watches and such. Just pretend you're in church; then your little offering won't hurt so much!" He laughed again.

Longarm was squatting beside the Russian woman who'd tumbled into the aisle when the train had screeched to a stop. While the woman grunted and groaned, Longarm

29

whipped looks out the soot-streaked windows, trying to determine how many desperadoes had waylaid the train. There had to be more than three.

"Hey, you in the cheap suit!"

Longarm looked at the man with the rifle, fifteen yards away and moving toward him slowly, swinging his bag from right to left as folks on both sides of the aisle made their "contributions." The desperado scowled at Longarm, aiming his rifle at the lawman's head, his lips bunched, his small green eyes slitted.

"Have a seat and get out your valuables," he barked. "And don't even think about goin' for that cross-draw six-shooter. You so much as touch the grips, I'll furnish you with a third eye free of charge."

"Just helpin' the lady to her seat," Longarm said, giving the Russian woman's thick right arm a tug as he rose.

When the sobbing woman was back in her seat with the little boy, Longarm stepped across the aisle and sank into his seat beside Miss Gandy.

"You're a real fucking gentleman, Cheap Suit," said the desperado, still waving the sack from right to left as he continued moving down the aisle, accepting wallets, coins, pocket watches, jewelry, and loose greenbacks. "I'll get to you in a minute, so get your valuables out like everyone else."

Longarm stared at the gent and slowly lifted his left hand toward his inside coat pocket, where his wallet resided. His right hand was twitching, inching slowly toward the walnut grips of his Colt .44.

He didn't want to make any sudden moves. A lead swap in such close quarters was liable to get a passenger greased. He'd let the man come right up on him; then, while the hardcase was distracted with another passenger, he'd make his move.

As he was wondering how many other robbers were in the group and where they were on the train, he heard the door at the opposite end of the coach squawk open and slam closed. Longarm turned to see another of the three "waddies" from the depot stop before the door to the outside platform, and raise a feed sack in his left hand while aiming a Winchester with his right.

"Lookee here, Donny-boy!" a man shouted behind Longarm. "My sack's half-full, and there's a wallet in here with five hundred dollars in it!"

The man ahead of Longarm stopped suddenly and cast a nostril-flared glare at the newcomer. "Goddamn you, Pig-Eye, we ain't s'posed to use each other's *real* names, you stupid son of a bitch!"

"How were they s'posed to know that was your real name till *you* told 'em?"

"Shut up and keep fillin' your sack." Donny swung his feed sack toward a young half-breed in a shabby wool coat two rows up from Longarm and on the left side of the aisle.

Watching Donny but keeping Pig-Eye in the periphery of his vision, Longarm removed his wallet from his inside coat pocket.

Miss Gandy placed her left hand on his forearm. Her hand was quivering, as was her voice as she whispered, "Aren't you going to do something?"

Keeping his eyes on Donny, Longarm opened his right hand to her. She removed her hand from his forearm, placed it in her lap with the other, and sat tensely, swinging her wide-eyed gaze from one desperado to the other.

"Come on, Cheap Suit. Drop your donation into the sack."

Donny stood before Longarm, curling his lips and aiming the rifle at Longarm's belly. The deputy rarely wore his badge except when issuing writs or making arrests, and he wasn't wearing it now. Good thing too. If these two knew he was a lawman, they'd have probably drilled him by now. He'd decided not to let them in on his secret until he was ready and the passengers were out of the way.

As Longarm raised his wallet toward Donny's sack, the desperado jerked his rifle at him and spat through gritted teeth, "And don't get funny either. I know you cardsharps carry plenty of cash. Show me your money belt!"

As he dropped his wallet into the feed sack, Longarm opened his mouth to tell the man he wasn't wearing a money belt this trip, but Miss Gandy cut him off. "How dare you speak to him that way!" she shrieked. "This man is a United States marshal, and he will not put up with being addressed in that manner, much less let you rob us all blind and do God knows what to us ladies!"

Donny slid his gaze from the girl to Longarm. His mustachioed lips stretched back from his mouth, revealing chipped, tobacco-stained teeth. "A lawman, eh? I thought I smelled somethin' rotten."

Longarm slid his gaze to Miss Gandy. "Thanks, miss. 'Preciate the help."

The desperado called Pig-Eye moved up on Longarm's left, squinting his right eye, which was slightly larger and set lower than the other beside the thick, pitted wedge of his nose. "Well, I'll be damned. You know who that is, Donny?"

Donny was grinning at Longarm, keeping his Winchester's barrel aimed at the deputy's chest. "Who?"

"That's Deputy United States Marshal Custis Long, known hereabouts as Longarm. He's out of Chief Marshal Vail's office in Denver. Mean son of a bitch. Merciless."

"Ah, shucks, I have *some* mercy," said Longarm.

"Well, I'll be damned." Donny shoved his feed sack at Pig-Eye, and raised his rifle to his shoulder. "I never killed a lawman before, but I reckon if I have to kill one, it might as well be a famous one. I'll have my name in all the papers."

"Wait a minute," Pig-Eye said, holding his rifle under one shoulder as he clutched the two feed sacks in his hands. "Are you sure you wanna do that?"

"Why the hell not? He's a lawman, ain't he?"

Pig-Eye shifted his pig-eyed gaze between Donny and Longarm. "I don't know. Shootin' a lawman—and one so damn famous—makes me kinda nervous. We're gonna have one hell of a high *re*-ward on our heads."

"So? If there's as much *dinero* on this train as Rooster said there was, we'll be headin' to Mexico."

Pig-Eye chuckled and shifted his weight from one foot to the other. "Hell, I reckon we can at that." He raised the two sacks in his hands. "We got enough cash right here, and T-Bob and Rooster are helpin' themselves to the loot in the express car."

As if to validate Pig-Eye's statement, the coach floor rocked beneath Longarm's boots, and a sudden thunderclap sounded. Or what sounded like a thunderclap. Longarm had heard enough dynamite detonations to know the gang had just blown the express car's safe.

The smell of cordite drifted through the coach's open windows. Pig-Eye sniffed and grinned. "That'd be them now."

Donny stared down his rifle barrel at Longarm. "Just let me drill this son of a bitch, and we'll split-ass outta here."

"Oh, my God!" Miss Gandy squeaked. "You *can't* kill him!"

Donny jerked the rifle toward her. "Shut up or I'll kill you too."

Miss Gandy's mouth had opened to exclaim once more, but she snapped it shut so suddenly that her teeth clacked.

Longarm raised his hands, palm out. "Hold on, boys. If you're gonna shoot me, shoot me outside, will you?"

Donny blinked. "Huh?"

"If you shoot me in here, your slug could ricochet off one of my tough old bones, and kill an innocent bystander."

Donny laughed. "I'll be real careful."

Pig-Eye nudged Donny's arm and glanced at the young woman clutching a toddler to her breast directly behind Longarm. "Come on, Donny. What harm could it do?"

Donny looked at the young woman and wide-eyed youngster on her lap. He cursed, grabbed Longarm's .44

from its cross-draw holster, and stuffed it behind his own cartridge belt. "Get to your feet and be quick about it. Any funny business, I'll drill you right here and I'll shoot one of these innocent *bystandards*!"

"Deputy Long!" Miss Gandy cried, clutching Longarm's bicep. "They're gonna kill you, and it's all on account of me!"

"Shut up, you little bitch!" Donny shouted, aiming the rifle at the girl while shoving Longarm toward the car's rear door. "Another word out of you, and I'll drill a hole through your head!"

The girl shrieked and covered her head with her arms.

Shoving Longarm forward with his rifle barrel, Donny told Pig-Eye to finish fleecing the passengers and meet him outside. Then he gave Longarm another shove, a prod between Longarm's shoulder blades. It wasn't much of a shove, but Longarm bent forward and faked a stumble down the aisle. At the same time, he lowered his right hand, as if to catch himself if he fell, and smoothly plucked his gold-plated derringer from his vest pocket.

Hiding the deadly little peashooter in his palm, Longarm raised his right hand to the door frame wall, bracing himself as he opened the door.

"Nice and slow," Donny ordered.

As he stepped through the door, Longarm cast a glance behind. Donny was about four feet off his heels, rifle raised. Longarm turned right and strode slowly down the steps to the ground, where he stopped and, holding his hands above his head, glanced behind him.

Donny was at the top of the steps between the coach cars. Grinning from ear to ear, the hardcase raised his rifle to his shoulder and squinted down the barrel. "Don't go tellin' St. Pete that Donny Childress didn't grant your last wish, lawma—"

Donny jerked his head up when he saw the derringer in Longarm's fist. *"Fuck!"*

34

As Donny snapped his cheek back down to the rifle's stock, Longarm triggered the derringer.

Pop!

A neat round hole appeared in Donny's left temple. As Donny flew straight back, he triggered the rifle in the air before throwing it out behind him. The long gun bounced off the front coach, shattering a bracket lamp, and disappeared down the other side of the train.

"What the *hell*!" Pig-Eye shouted inside the coach. The car rocked as Pig-Eye's boots pounded down the aisle.

Longarm leaped toward the steps, intending to grab his double-action .44 from behind Donny's cartridge belt. Another rifle cracked. Longarm stopped with one boot on the bottom step.

A rider galloped toward him along the stalled cars—a mustachioed gent dressed as roughly as Donny and Pig-Eye, and aiming a Spencer carbine one-handed, head bobbing as his horse loped past the coal tender.

The rider snapped off another shot, the slug blowing up sand from the cinder bed. His right boot still on the car's bottom step, Longarm turned toward the car. In the rearmost window, a shadow flickered as Pig-Eye's footfalls grew louder.

A half second later, Pig-Eye dashed through the car's rear door. Longarm cursed under his breath, ducked under the coach, and crawled on hands and knees over the rails to the other side.

Pig-Eye's shout rose from the platform. "Where are you, ye son of a bitch!"

Longarm straightened on the other side of the coach, sidled up to the platform. Pig-Eye had dropped both loot bags at his feet. Facing the rear coach, he cocked the revolvers in his hands as he looked off the opposite side of the train from Longarm.

"Drop it or die, Pig-Eye!" Longarm ordered behind him, raising the derringer.

Pig-Eye swung his head around, eyes snapping wide. As he began swinging his right Remy toward Longarm, the lawman drilled a hole through the middle of Pig-Eye's chest. Pig-Eye screamed and flew down the steps, skipping a slug off the top step with an angry, sparking roar.

Pig-Eye hadn't disappeared before the rider shot into view between the cars, drawing his horse to a skidding halt with one hand while aiming the carbine through the gap.

Longarm ducked as the carbine spoke.

The slug plunked into a telegraph pole behind him. Turning, he tripped over his own feet and rolled down the railroad bed. He lay at the embankment's base for a moment, blinking.

He turned his head. Two feet from his left cheek lay Donny's rifle, which must have slid down the bed when Donny had thrown it off the train. Longarm grabbed it, rose to a knee, and rammed a shell into the rifle's breech, casting a glance at the coach.

The rider now crouched on the platform over Donny's lifeless body, his carbine aimed at Longarm.

The gun boomed.

The slug tore into the rocks over Longarm's right shoulder.

Longarm snapped Donny's rifle up and fired. The man on the platform grunted and, dropping his rifle and losing his hat, clutched his right shoulder. He clutched at the rail for a second, cursing, then dropped out of sight.

To Longarm's left, hooves thundered. Above the thunder, a man shouted, "Goddamnit! What the fuck's goin' on?"

Ramming a fresh shell into the Winchester's breech, Longarm swung the gun on the three riders pounding toward him, angling away from the express car with a smoking, gaping hole in its side. Two of the riders fired at Longarm at the same time, one slug barking off a rock to Longarm's left, another plunking into the gravel two feet in front of him.

Longarm snapped off a quick shot, then wheeled and

36

ran away from the train as three more bullets stitched the air around his head.

He zigzagged around two boulders, and suddenly the ground fell out from under his feet. Being otherwise occupied, he hadn't realized the train had been traversing the shoulder of a rocky hill when the owlhoots had stopped it. Rolling down the brushy incline, sand and gravel flying, his hat tumbling off his head, the rifle skidding down the hill behind him, he glimpsed a deep-cut creek bed below.

He dropped down a steep trough, hit the ground below with a deep *whuhhh!* as the air was hammered from his lungs. Bending his knees and sucking air down his windpipe, he looked up.

The trough he'd just fallen down was the steepest part of the hill. Above, the three horsemen were thundering toward him—two to the left of the trough, the other to the right. Their pistols and rifles popped, the slugs plunking into the gravel and rabbit brush surrounding Longarm.

Sucking a deep breath, the lawman bounded to his knees, grabbed the rifle, brushed sand from the breech, and levered a shell.

The ground shuddered as the three horsemen approached. Triggering a shot at the single rider, Longarm leapt forward and pumped his arms and legs toward the creek.

A bullet clipped his heel. The boot shot out from beneath him. He hit the ground on his right shoulder, and turned to face the horses.

The riders were twenty yards away and closing.

As one of the men on the left whooped with glee and triggered a Buntline Special, Longarm fired the rifle. The Buntline-wielding owlhoot screamed and rolled off his horse's back, dropping the long-barreled revolver, blood spraying from his neck.

His rifle's report hadn't ceased echoing before Longarm rolled over the lip of the creek and into the bed, twisting and setting both feet down in the soft, red clay. At the same time, he lifted the Winchester's barrel over the lip of the

37

bank, fired left, then, ejecting the smoking shell as he swung the barrel right, fired again.

The man on his right winced and sagged over his right stirrup fender, dropping both his pistols.

Longarm glanced to his left. The rider over there had fallen out of his saddle. His right boot had hung up in his stirrup, and he was bouncing along the ground as the horse, propelled by its own momentum, plunged over the creek bank.

"Ohhhh . . . *ahhhhh*!" the owlhoot screamed as he careened out over the bank to Longarm's left, boot still soundly gripped by the flapping stirrup, the poor bastard's arms waving as though he were trying to take flight.

Longarm didn't see the horse and rider hit the creek bed. Spying the other horse bearing down on him, he turned to his right. His eyes snapped wide.

The horse had swerved away from the creek, unseating its rider. The big man bounced along the ground as though shot from a cannon . . .

And headed straight for Longarm.

The lawman had only begun to dodge when the man's torso flew over the lip of the bank. The body hit Longarm so hard that time skipped ahead several seconds. Longarm stared straight up into the faultless blue sky. What felt like two hundred pounds of grain pressed down on his chest, squeezing his lungs.

His vision swam. He blinked, glanced over his right shoulder.

The big man's head lay in the sand and gravel, face turned toward Longarm. The eyes were open, glassy in death. Blood trickled down both corners of his mouth. The man's body, lying crossways atop Longarm's, twitched eerily, the legs sliding as if trying to run.

Longarm drew a pinched breath, lifted his head, and tried to push the big carcass off his chest. But his arms felt light as feather dusters, and his head sagged back to the sand.

As if from far away, he heard running footsteps. "Deputy Long! Deputy Long! Oh, God, are you *dead*?"

Longarm looked up, squinted as he tried to get the creek bed to stop pitching from side to side. Miss Gandy swam into view, standing at the lip of the creek bank, staring down at him, hatless, hair hanging in loose curls about her slender shoulders. She wrung her hands together.

"Deputy Long!" she cried again, sobbing.

Two men appeared on either side of her—one dressed in greasy denim coveralls, another dressed in conductor's blues with a leather-billed hat. The conductor had a fat lip and a swollen left eye.

Both men climbed awkwardly down the bank. The engineer rolled the dead man off Longarm's chest while the conductor, pinching his trousers up his thighs and dropping to one knee, stared into the lawman's eyes.

"Custis? I say there, Custis, are you still among the living?"

Longarm stretched his lips back as he remembered the conductor's name—Noble Price. He'd punched more than a few of the lawman's train tickets over the years.

Longarm rose to his elbows and spat grit from his lips. He looked at the girl, still staring worriedly down at him. "Miss Gandy," he said, "next time Ugly Jim Finn comes callin', do me a favor?"

"What's that, Deputy Long?"

"Keep your consarned mouth shut!"

Chapter 5

Nothing wreaked havoc on train schedules like brush fires and holdups.

By the time Longarm and the train crew had loaded the bodies of the dead owlhoots in a stock car, and had cleared from the rails the burning timber the gang had used to stop the flier with, they were nearly two hours behind schedule. At the site of the holdup, they were a half hour from Colorado Springs, and while the train chugged through the rocky foothills in the shadow of snow-mantled Pikes Peak, the passengers—including Longarm and Miss Gandy—reappropriated their stolen possessions from the robbers' burlap sacks. The big Russian woman kissed Longarm's cheek and patted his butt with gratitude, and he was clapped on the shoulders and back by the other passengers and crew until he thought his spine would crack. Miss Gandy, owly since he'd yelled at her down in the creek bed, gave him the cold shoulder.

She was no happier about the additional delay in Colorado Springs. Longarm killed another hour conferring with the town marshal, Fulton T. Myers, filling out the necessary forms and affidavits that are the bane of any lawman—especially *federal* lawmen—mixed up in a killing. He also scrawled a report to Billy Vail in Denver. Marshal Myers assured Longarm that he'd cable the report to Billy as soon as the telegraph wires, which the gang had cut, had been repaired.

The marshal and his three deputies had no trouble identifying the dead owlhoots. To a man, they were all drovers who'd worked for various spreads in the region for the past ten or fifteen years. The marshal was surprised to learn that Rooster Grange, Pig-Eye Kroeger, and their compatriots had taken to riding the long coulees.

But then, it took a stalwart sort of brush-popper to resign himself to thirty-a-month-and-found until he was too stove up to ride a horse anymore. Or until he'd been kicked in the head one too many times and was cut from a ranch roll to die alone in some abandoned fur trapper's shack, or howling and yowling with syphilis in a whore's crib.

Longarm had done them all a favor, Marshal Myers concluded, nodding and shaking Longarm's hand as he ushered the deputy U.S. marshal and his pouting charge, Miss Gandy, onto the narrow-gauge Central City line as cool, purple shadows slid down from the jagged western peaks.

"Good luck in Lulu City," the marshal said to Longarm.

To Miss Gandy, heading for one of the hard wooden bench seats on the right side of the spartan, toylike coach, Myers added, "Oh, and ma'am, you shouldn't suffer any more impositions on this run. Those owlhoots that been plaguing your father's gold shipments only strike when the train's comin' *down* from Lulu City to Colorado Springs. You'll be rattling along *empty to* Lulu City, sure enough! Good luck and bye now!"

Not long after Myers had left, and Longarm and Miss Gandy had made themselves as comfortable as possible on the bench seats, the train rattled westward out of Colorado Springs.

Soon they seemed to be climbing straight up through high, pine-studded passes, the cold mountain air pushing

41

against the grimy windows and straining the heating abilities of the charcoal braziers at either end of the coach, which was filled with the typical mining camp fare of pimps, gamblers, pleasure girls, and whiskey drummers. Beyond the frosted windows, the night was too dark for Longarm to see much but the snowy slopes glowing like a child's Christmas dream in the glistening starlight.

Longarm saw no reason not to break the ice again with Miss Gandy. After all, they'd be stuck together in the same coach—one of only two coaches on the entire narrow-gauge squawker—as well as the same seat.

"Sorry I yelled at you," he said, nudging her shoulder with his arm. When she made no response, he added in spite of himself—in spite of his many scrapes and bruises and his sore head, "I reckon I might've overreacted some."

She made a show of yawning and loudly turning a page of the thick tome by Henry James.

She made no other effort to communicate for the next twenty-four hours, until the second night, when the train was squawking and rattling and chugging up another in a long line of infernal, twisting, seemingly endless rocky saddles.

"I simply must sleep," she groaned, squirming around in her seat, adjusting the two Hudson Bay blankets she'd wrapped herself in after leaving Colorado Springs.

She dropped her book to the floor and turned to Longarm. She'd removed her hat, and her hair was rumpled, her cheeks flushed, her lips pooched out. She looked more vulnerable and appealing now than she did when Longarm had first spied her, a haughty little ringtail reading her Henry James in the train station. "May I rest my head on your lap? I've scouted both coach cars, and there are absolutely no spare benches."

"Uh . . ."

"Please, Deputy Long. If I don't get my rest—and I've gone entirely too long without sleep the way it is—I'll come apart at the seams."

"Well, then . . . I reckon." Longarm moved the butt of his Colt out of the way and adjusted his legs. Before he knew it, she'd kicked her own feet onto the bench and collapsed her head onto his lap.

"Why not?" he added, as if reassuring himself it would not be a problem.

He hadn't sat with a woman's head on his lap for a long time, and when he had, the head had usually belonged to a woman he'd frolicked with in his birthday suit. So becoming aroused was no problem. But in Miss Gandy's case, if he wasn't chaste in his thoughts, the quickening of his incorrigible male juices could get downright embarrassing.

He shifted his butt a little, so that her head rested on his right thigh. He'd no sooner made the adjustment than she lifted up, giving a little grunt, and snuggled her head down in the hollow *between* his thighs, where it was no doubt more comfortable. At least for her.

She turned sideways, curled her legs beneath the blankets, and snugged her right hand on his knee, turning her head again to snuggle deeper into the hollow.

Her cheek and hand instantly warmed him. To distract himself from the sensation, which would have aroused any male with a pulse, he looked out the window.

All he could see was starlight flickering behind the frosted glass.

Shit.

Well, hell, he'd just go to sleep.

He looked around the car, lit by only the coal stoves and a couple of guttering, smoking bracket lamps, the other passengers slouched in silhouette, then rested his head against the seat back.

He tipped his hat brim low and closed his eyes.

He focused on the darkness behind his lids, relaxed into the slow-moving train's jostles and sways. Taking a deep breath, he relaxed his shoulders.

The girl moved her head around on his lap, gave a little groan.

Longarm tried to ignore the tickling of his privates. He tried instead to focus on the problem he'd be facing once he made it to Lulu City.

Nasty bunch of outlaws. The Holy Smokes Gang would make the train robbers he'd run into earlier look like children with wooden pistols playing holdup on the school playground. . . .

The girl lifted her head slightly, said softly, almost inaudibly above the train's creaks and squeaks and the thunderous snores of a pimp sitting directly ahead of Longarm, "Would you please slide your revolver aside, Deputy Long? It's hard beneath my head."

Longarm jerked his head down. His face turned instantly hot as he realized his shaft was at half-mast under his trousers, straining his fly buttons and drawing his underwear taut.

He shifted, trying to maneuver the offending rod from the girl's face. This, however, was not going to work. Billy Vail should try sitting cool as a parson while a girl cuddled his privates.

"Tell you what, miss—I'll go make myself comfortable out on the platform between the cars, and you can take a nap."

He placed his hands on the bench, ready to rise, but she didn't lift her head as he'd expected. Instead, she turned completely around to face him, and drew the blankets over her head.

For a few seconds, it felt as though a mouse was gnawing at his fly buttons.

Longarm felt his cock harden another quarter. He leaned forward. "Whoah, now. Miss Gandy . . ."

But her persistent fingers reached inside his fly hole, scuttled about his underwear for nearly a minute before he felt her flesh on his—her fingertips sliding along the offending shaft until she'd filled her fist with it and was working the organ from its hole.

The maneuver was delightfully painful. Longarm gritted his teeth and looked around, hoping no one noticed the blankets moving around on his lap, grateful the lamp globes were too dirty to shed much light and that one lamp had burned down to a mere spark.

A giggle sounded . . . hopefully only to Longarm's ears.

His organ was out of his pants, standing straight up from the fly, the swollen head rubbing the blanket. Miss Gandy had one hand wrapped around it, and was turning it this way and that, gently, as if inspecting it. He felt the warm wetness of her tongue on its tip, then sliding slowly down the bottom side of the shaft toward his balls.

A boy's voice rose to his left. "Sandwich, mister?"

Longarm's eyes popped open. He tried to arrange a casual expression as he turned to regard the boy, seven or eight, in a ratty suit with knickers and a frayed bowler, standing before him. The lad held a newsprint-covered lump in one hand, a croaker sack in the other.

Miss Gandy had frozen with her face buried in Longarm's balls, one hand holding steady on his cock. Her body jerked as she giggled soundlessly.

Longarm found his tongue. "No, thanks, sonny."

"Fresh roast beef sandwich, sir. Only twenty-five cents, less'n you want a hot potato with it."

Longarm tried a smile. "Thanks, sonny. Just ain't hungry this evenin'."

He felt his organ begin to melt and his face grow hotter as the boy looked at the lumpy blanket on Longarm's lap. The blanket shook as the girl laughed, tonguing his cock to keep it stiff. Longarm doffed his hat, set it over Miss Gandy's head on his lap. He was glad the coach was good and dark.

The lad turned to Longarm with a perplexed wrinkle of his brow. "You all right, mister?"

"Just fine, sonny. Bringin' a puppy home to my daughter. He's just dreamin' while he sleeps under my hat."

"I seen you board with that girl, and I didn't see no puppy." The kid looked up and down the aisle. "Say, where *is* the girl? Do you think *she'd* like a sandwich?"

"She's just taking some air. I doubt she's hungry either. Train rides tend to make her vapory."

That seemed to satisfy the lad as far as Miss Gandy was concerned, but he remained where he was. "You *sure* you don't want a sandwich?"

"No, thanks, son." Longarm put some steel in his voice, though he kept the smile on his lips. "Run along now. I'm right sleepy."

The kid hiked a shoulder and, to Longarm's everlasting relief, drifted on up the coach to tap the sleeping pimp on the shoulder. At the same time, Miss Gandy went back to her bewitching industry beneath the blankets, and it was no time before she'd slipped her warm mouth over his fully erect organ once again, and was moving up and down.

Longarm was dumbstruck.

How could a girl so persnickety and innocent perform such a brash, subtle, expert maneuver?

Then it occurred to him that she wasn't nearly as innocent as she'd seemed. She *couldn't* be. All that time she'd spent at the teachers school, far from the watchful eye of her father, had not been devoted entirely to Mr. James and other dry-as-dust tomes, but most likely to some real-life adventures with the opposite sex on the wrong side of the tracks.

As her mouth suddenly slid over his throbbing organ, the lips soft and full, the tongue dancing back and forth along the shaft, Longarm reasoned that this was not her first French lesson. That became more and more obvious the longer she sucked, using her lips, tongue, and fingers. Like the deftest of doxies, she urged him on, then held him back, repeating the maneuver several times until he thought his heart would explode.

Finally, he drew a deep breath and held it, rising off the bench as his seed jetted down her opening and closing throat.

When he was finally spent, she tucked him back into his trousers, buttoned the fly, and drew the blankets away from her head. Her voice was at once girlish and husky. "Took care of that, didn't I?"

She chuckled, snuggled her head back down in his crotch. "Deputy Long?"

"Might as well call me Custis."

"Custis, how many owlhoots have you gunned, if you don't mind me asking?"

Longarm, still breathing hard, looked down at her. Her brown eyes stared back at him through the darkness. He'd never counted, but he chuckled and said, "Oh, a good hundred, most like."

She lifted her head slightly. "A hundred men! Really?"

"Give or take."

"Custis?"

He looked down at her again. "I wasn't mad before," she said. "I was just sorta . . . taken aback by what you did to those long-riders. Sorta took my breath away, I guess you could say. Mr. Dead-Eye Dick himself couldn't have written it any better."

Longarm kept his voice low, cleared the thickness from his throat. "Miss Gandy, where did you learn such a thing?"

"The French lesson? Well, I'm really not a very good student. Truth be known, I do prefer Dead-Eye Dick and Mr. Frank Leslie to Mr. James or any of his stuffy brethren. Doesn't seem to matter, though." She pinched her nose and snickered. "I treat the head schoolmaster just fine and get all A's!"

She rolled her cheek against the lawman's finally subdued organ. "Good night, Custis."

In a minute, he heard her regular, deep breaths beneath the snores from the slumbering pimp in the next seat up and the train's roar all around.

Miss Gandy rose from Longarm's lap about an hour after first light. She tossed the blankets away, as the morning sunshine had warmed the coach cars considerably.

"Good morning, Dep—" She stopped herself, blushing and lowering her eyes. "I mean, Custis."

"Miss Gandy," the lawman said, shuffling his feet to work some blood into his thighs. He'd risen twice to use the privy and to smoke cigars on the platform between coaches, but otherwise he'd spent the evening pinned beneath the girl's head.

"I reckon you might as well call me Rose."

"All right, Rose." Longarm grinned.

He'd been right. Having a pretty traveling companion had indeed added color to what might have been an otherwise dull train ride. She was prettier than what he'd originally thought, he noticed as she stared out the coach window, her cheeks fairly glowing in the sunlight. Her brown eyes were lustrous, and so was her hair, which hung in pretty, tussled locks to her shoulders.

Longarm just hoped her father didn't learn about his "trifling," as Billy Vail had put it, with the mine manager's daughter. But then, Longarm hadn't trifled with Miss Gandy. It had been the other way around. In fact, if a man had trifled so with a woman, he'd very likely be charged with rape!

"Here it is—we're there," Rose said as a rocky mountain fell away from the windows on both sides of the coach. A valley opened, bathed in golden, high-altitude sunshine, with stock corrals and warehouses lined along the tracks, shaft houses and ore tipples showing on the shouldering slopes of the mountains.

Rose adjusted her hat. "There's Papa."

"You don't sound too thrilled, Miss Rose."

"I love Papa dearly," the girl said with a sigh. "He's a good provider and a shrewd businessman, but I might as well tell you right now, Custis, Papa slaps the Bible about as hard as anyone you've probably ever met!"

Chapter 6

Chagrin was turning a man's daughter over to him after said daughter had just French-kissed your privates. Especially when said father, as Custis had so recently learned, was a God-fearing man.

"Rose!" barked the tall granite-faced gent, who looked more like an old fur trapper than a mine owner, waiting on the platform's brick cobbles while the locomotive chugged and panted like a winded dinosaur.

The bearded, burly man—clad in baggy denims and a sheepskin vest over a red-plaid shirt—removed the corncob pipe from his teeth, and thrust it into his pocket. Approaching Rose gravely, he took her hands in both of his, bowed his head, and, Rose automatically following suit, dropped to one knee.

"Our Father who art in heaven," Mr. Gandy said, eyes pinched closed, clasping his daughter's hands, "thank you for returning my daughter to me safely." He opened his eyes, regarded Rose expectantly. "Daughter?"

When Gandy had again lowered his head, Rose glanced over his shoulder at Longarm—a complicitous look of strained patience. She closed her eyes and dipped her chin to her chest. "Thank you, Lord, for returning me safely to

Papa. And thank you for keeping him healthy and well while I was away. He looks fit as ever, and I know he wouldn't be that way had you not been casting your gracious blessings down upon him."

Together, they said, "Amen."

Even then, there were no hugs or kisses. The way these two greeted each other, they could have been two members of the same church meeting for the first time. The old man didn't even crack a smile as he looked down at his daughter, plucking his pipe from his pocket.

"You been behavin' yourself in school, child?"

Rose straightened her hat and cast a sly glance at Longarm. Her voice was cool, subtly mocking. "You haven't had any letters from Superintendent Leonard, have you, Papa?"

The old man scowled. "Can't say as I have. And wouldn't expect to. I raised you right, didn't I?"

She glanced at Longarm again. "Butter wouldn't melt in my mouth, Papa."

The gent more resembled Jim Bridger than the dandified mine owner Longarm had expected to find here in Lulu City. He chuffed mirthlessly and tapped out the dottle from his pipe. "Don't know if I'd go that far, but I reckon I raised you as good as I could—just me an' ole Jehovah."

Longarm stood to one side, feeling like the new kid in class while puffing his cigar and holding the girl's portmanteau in one hand, his own war bag and rifle in the other.

"God-fearin'—that's me, Papa," Rose said, a mocking glint in her eyes as she turned to indicate Longarm with her open hand.

"Solomon Gandy, meet my chaperone, Deputy United States Marshal Custis Long."

"So they did send only one man," Gandy scoffed as, shaking Longarm's hand, he glanced around the cobbles as if hoping to see more badge-toters. "Marshal Vail said they were just gonna send one, but I hoped he'd change his mind."

Before Longarm could respond, Rose smiled primly at him and said, "He saved my life, you know."

Gandy's small, gray eyes grew skeptical.

"Sure enough," Rose said. "We were attacked by a pack of vicious owlhoots halfway between Denver and Colorado Springs. Deputy Long here, more commonly known as Longarm, promptly cleaned the clocks of the entire gang. *Single-handedly!*"

"What's this?" Mr. Gandy said, glowering at Longarm disbelievingly.

"Pow! Pow! Pow!" Rose said, narrowing her eyes at Longarm, her cheeks flushed as if she were reliving the entire episode. A wolfish grin spread her lips. "And when the dust settled, the entire gang of six lay dead in the bloody dirt!"

"Now, the dirt wasn't all *that* bloody, Miss Rose," Longarm pointed out.

Gandy frowned down at his daughter. "Are you all right, Rose?"

"I came through unscathed, Papa. Thanks to the good deputy here."

"Just a band of brush-popping cow waddies that got tired of bunkhouse grub," Longarm said. "As the marshal of Colorado Springs pointed out, they've gone to a better place. Enough about them, Mr. Gandy. I'm here about the Hawk Haughton Gang and your ravaged gold shipments."

"In due time, Marshal. We'll discuss the situation at my cabin, if that's agreeable. My mine superintendent and the freight company's foreman will join us after breakfast. They'd join us now, but both had other appointments."

"However you want to do it," Longarm said as they entered the small, brick depot building. "Is this a safe place to store my war bag and rifle for a few hours, Mr. Gandy?"

"Safe as any in town."

The big man grabbed Longarm's rifle and war bag, and strolled up to the ticket cage. Behind the rough pine counter, a thin gent in spats and armbands was writing out tickets for a pair of husky Germans in hobnailed boots and duck coats and smoking hand-carved pipes as they pontificated quietly in their native tongue.

The thin gent noticed Gandy immediately, and snapped to Gandy's attention. He relieved the big, stern man of the war bag and rifle, then bowed like a Chinaman while assuring the mine owner of the articles' safety. Holding the war bag and rifle as though they were the emperor's family diamonds, he disappeared into a paneled back room.

Gandy returned to Longarm and Rose. "Safe as in any bank in Denver City," the miner proudly intoned, taking his daughter's right elbow. "The Hawk Haughton Gang might mess with my gold down canyon, but no one trifles with me in town. Without me, the town wouldn't even be here!"

Gandy led the way outside. A small platform spring dray sat near a hitch rack and a dirty, knee-high snowbank, a Cordovan mule in the traces. The big man set Rose's portmanteau in the back, then tossed his daughter into the driver's box as though she weighed little more than a box of buckwheat cereal.

Casting a passing, preliminary glance around the humble main drag, with its usual collection of false-fronted buildings spewing pine-scented wood smoke—most whipsawed and still smelling strongly of pine resin—Longarm climbed aboard the wagon from the opposite side.

He wasn't paying very close attention to the little mining camp, however. Gandy himself was too puzzling. Few gold barons dressed as though they were still breaking rock themselves. And why wheel around in a rustic, mud-splattered spring dray when Gandy could no doubt afford a leather-seated surrey?

While Longarm was wondering if he'd been given the name of the wrong contact here in Lulu City, Gandy loosed a bellow. The mule bolted away from the boardwalk and snowdrift, and shot down the manure-covered street still spotted with occasional snowbanks and muddy rivulets.

The big animal gave a couple of halfhearted brays as Gandy steered around ore wagons, berated jaywalkers, splashed through snowmelt mud puddles, and took the first right turn around an ornate, three-story structure painted green and gold and calling itself THE LONDON HOTEL.

Longarm clutched the seat with one hand, his hat with the other, as the mule and wagon shot up a steep hill, leaving the town's low-roofed shacks quickly behind. Along the rocky, snow-spotted slopes rising in the north and west were strewn the trailings and overburdens of several mine tunnels.

Smoke and steam rose from behind a rimrock, no doubt from a mine works and a stamping mill. Huge firewood and ore wagons threaded the ridges. Longarm heard the monotonous clank of a stamping mill's iron pistons turning ore into workable dust.

Beneath it rose the yells of teamsters, the clatter and squawk of the wagons, and the indignant brays of the mules.

If all that commotion was from Solomon Gandy's Holy Smokes Mine, it was a sizable operation indeed.

Longarm braced his boots on the dashboard as the wagon curved through pine- and cedar-studded buttes, then rumbled to a halt in the yard of a dilapidated, story-and-a-half log shanty with a single, transplanted spruce growing just right of the front, Z-frame door.

A large, flat-topped boulder with a crack down the middle fronted the hovel. Atop the boulder was a wicker chair facing west, and a dozen black cigar stubs.

Behind the cabin stood a two-horse stable constructed of vertical planks, a corral of unpeeled pine logs, and a chicken coop. A windmill turned lazily, squeaking. The whole yard, spotted with snow, was set on the slant of the ridge, so that an earthquake or rock slide might sweep the cabin, barn, and stable into the little town four hundred yards below.

Rose must have seen Longarm's look of puzzlement as he swept his eyes about the grounds.

"Papa's original shack when he first started digging here twenty years ago," she said, as Gandy wrapped the reins around the brake handle, then reached up to help her down. "You'd think he'd build something bigger and more stylish." Rose chuckled. "Not Papa. That'd be too extravagant."

She leaned toward the brusque man and, to Longarm's surprise, planted a kiss on his weathered, bearded cheek. There was no mocking glance to undercut it either. However strained their relationship might have been, the girl loved the man.

Other than to flush slightly, Gandy did not react to the kiss. His low voice rumbled softly. "Extravagance is a sin, daughter. You know that."

He glanced at Longarm, his eyes proud. "Truth be told, my first cabin was down along the creek. Little more than stones and brush me and my old partner, Cherokee St. George, threw together when we were still just shoveling out cracks and panning the dirt out in the creek. No white man within a hundred miles back then."

Gandy threw out a hand to indicate the cabin, a thin ribbon of blue smoke rising from the field-rock chimney abutting the east wall. "Compared to that, this here's a Jay Gould mansion."

Gandy had set Rose's portmanteau on the rock-mounted cabin stoop, and was gathering split logs in his arms while Longarm stood, thumbs in his cartridge belt, looking around. Two graves, half-covered with icy, dirty snow, had been marked off by rocks a few feet to the west and up a low rise trimmed with cedars.

"That's where Momma and Cherokee St. George are buried," Rose said.

"Influenza," Gandy said, awkwardly tripping the door latch and kicking the door open, his arms full of wood. "That consarned fever took 'em both the same year, three

54

years after Rose was born. I raised this girl with one hand and slung a nine-pound hammer with the other."

He crouched through the doorway, dumped the wood in a box beside the fireplace, then turned to Longarm with one eye squinted. "I ain't complainin', you understand. It was God's will."

He cast his gaze about the room. "Make yourself at home, Deputy. Have that chair in the corner. Built it myself, stuffed it with horsehair, and stretched a prime bighorn sheep pelt over the top. The horns on the arms there are his too. Damn near had to fight a mountain lion for him before I finally got him to the cabin. I prayed and I prayed, and, with God's help, I finally got him home."

Gandy was shoving wood into the fireplace, blue smoke billowing and sparks popping.

Longarm sagged into the deep chair, which felt like a cloud after the hard oak train bench, his eyes wandering the room filled with rough-hewn but comfortable furniture, game trophies on the walls, pelts on the floor, and a kitchen space in the back, where a narrow staircase rose to the second story.

A small, wood-burned plaque hung on the wall over the fireplace: THE LORD IS MY SHEPHERD. Another, on the adjacent wall, read, BLESSED IS THE MAN WHO ENDURETH TEMPTATION.

Gandy asked Rose if she felt up to helping him cook breakfast after her long trip. She replied by favoring the man's leathery cheek with another soft kiss. "I won't only help, I'll do it all myself. You sit down over there with Longarm, and I'll get you men some coffee shortly."

Gandy flushed and glanced with embarrassment at the lawman. "Glad she ain't been spoiled by them Eastern ways. I been worried about that."

Longarm's face heated up as, donning an apron, Rose snickered quietly and worked the pump handle at an iron sink equipped with hollow logs through which waste water could run through the east wall and outside. A handy contraption. It appeared as though Gandy was not only frugal and pious, but self-sufficient.

"Did she say 'Longarm'?" Gandy asked, eyeing the lawman skeptically as he plopped his big frame into a deep leather chair.

"That's what most folks call me. Long arm of the law, or some such nonsense." Longarm turned now to look out the window behind him, where the smoke spewed toward the high, pine-studded ridges. "I take your mine's up thataway, Mr. Gandy? Behind that rimrock? For future reference, you understand. I'll have to pay a visit later."

"Just over the rise to the west. 'The Holy Smokes,' I call it, on account of when I realized the size of the vein I'd suddenly tapped into—after five hard years of drilling and picking and blasting—I took off my hat, held it over my heart, and said with utter humility, 'Holy smokes.' Said it again after I had the ore assayed and found out it ran three thousand dollars to the ton."

Longarm blinked. "Throw that to me slower so's I can catch it with my hat."

"You heard right," Gandy said, scratching a lucifer to life on his thumbnail. "Three thousand to the ton. It's some paler now, but not by much."

"Heck, Mr. Gandy, you could have a mansion up yonder and use this here cabin to stable your favorite *Thoroughbred stallion*!"

Gandy grimaced as he puffed his pipe. "You sound like my daughter."

"You could at that, Papa," Rose agreed from the kitchen, where she was cutting thick wedges of bacon into grease popping in a cast-iron skillet. "You could employ a woman to cook for you full-time, and a couple of men to cut and chop your wood so you wouldn't give yourself a heart seizure."

"Listen to that. Rose'd have me in a silk smoking jacket and layin' abed all day playin' euchre with the stable boys.

56

I preached the Bible to her all the years she was growin' up—we didn't have any bona fide men of the cloth up here back then, though we have one now—and she still don't understand that those ways lead to sin." Gandy shook his head and regarded his daughter darkly. "Troubles me, it does. . . ."

"I'm just funnin' you, Papa," Rose said, gently cajoling, her back turned.

Longarm was beginning to see why Rose was on the lusty side. Growing up out here with old Solomon Gandy and the Golden Rule probably hadn't been a whole lot of fun for a passionate, imaginative girl. She'd probably been eager to get away from home, and was damn sure enjoying her freedom.

Gandy sucked his pipe for a time. "I know you're anxious to get on the job, Deputy Long. I'm anxious to have that gang run to ground. But let's wait and talk business after breakfast." He touched his stomach and made a sour face, holding his pipe to the side of his mouth. "That demon-spawned Hawk Haughton Bunch gives me a sour stomach, and besides, Rose is too timid for such dark palaver."

"Timid," Longarm said, covering his blush with a yawn and bouncing his hat on his knee. Rose tossed him a smirk from the stove. "I knew she was right timid from the first I spied her, Mr. Gandy. You raised her right!"

"Here they are now, right on time," Solomon Gandy said when they'd finished breakfast and Rose was clearing the dishes. The big mine owner had craned his head to stare out the sashed window behind him. He turned to Rose. "Your beau's here, Rose."

The girl turned from the sink to the window, swept a curtain back with her right hand. Longarm, at the opposite end of the table from Gandy, stared past Rose at the two wagons climbing the grade on the two-track trail.

Both wagons were fine wood and leather, the second

with a tasseled canopy and a fine blue roan in the traces. Longarm turned his head to look through the front windows as the wagons pulled to the hitch rack. The first wagon was driven by a rangy gent with a spade beard and a black patch over his right eye. On the seat beside him sat a stocky, sandy-haired younker, a leather briefcase on his knees, reading a paper held close to his face.

The two men in the first wagon and the single gent in the second were all dressed impeccably, like city businessmen—fine broadcloth and silk, with beaver hats and polished patent leather shoes.

Longarm was still trying to get his mind around what Gandy had just said. "Did you say Rose's *beau* is here, Mr. Gandy?"

"Sure enough," Gandy said as Rose, wiping her hands on her apron, hurried across the living room to the front door. "One of them dandies is the foreman for the freight company that hauls my gold down to the main line at Colorado Springs. The blond shaver superintends my mine and, for better or worse, is my future son-in-law."

Chapter 7

Staring out the window at Rose's stocky young beau, Longarm considered that he was about to occupy the same small cabin with two men who had reason to kill him. But hell, he'd faced worse odds. It was Billy Vail's wrath he was worried about.

Across the table, Solomon Gandy wiped his mouth with a blue-checked napkin, rose from his chair, and strode across the living room to the front door.

Rose had already stepped out.

Through the right front window, Longarm watched the short, broad-shouldered, sandy-haired gent take Rose in his arms and, while he did not kiss her in front of her father, he squeezed her so tight he no doubt got a good feel of whatever breasts she might have under her school-marm's corset.

In spite of himself, Longarm had been curious about those ever since the surprisingly good French lesson in the narrow-gauge coach. But he'd probably found out as much about Rose as he ever would.

While Rose and the sandy-haired gent—who couldn't have been much over twenty, with apple cheeks and a double-dimpled grin—cavorted outside, holding hands and grinning at each other like love-struck schoolkids, Gandy ushered the other two gents into the kitchen, where he introduced them to Longarm.

The man with the spade beard and eye patch who'd been driving the first wagon was the sandy-haired gent's secretary. Longarm thought he looked more like a professional gambler or gunslinger than a pencil-sharpener. He also looked vaguely familiar, though Longarm, feeling instinctively suspicious of the man, couldn't place him. His handle was Phil Yoakum.

The second man—pudgy and sweaty, with little, colorless eyes set close to his pug nose—looked exactly like what he was, foreman for the freight company. Boyd Spandhauer's handshake was soft and wet as white bread dough, and his smile showed a full set of small, square teeth only slightly discolored by coffee and tobacco.

Gandy, Yoakum, Spandhauer, and Longarm had just sat down and filled their own coffee cups when Rose led the sandy-haired lad in by the hand, both looking as flustered as Longarm had no doubt been when Rose had dropped her thin, soft lips over his cock.

"Ah, here he is," Gandy said, blowing on his coffee. "Manager of the Holy Smokes Mine, Mr. Ebeneezer T. Coleridge. Still wet behind the ears, but God-fearin', mind you, and I'll be doggoned if he can't organize men and equipment and order supplies. Rose, why don't you go on upstairs and catch some shut-eye? You can clean up after our powwow."

"Papa, I'd like to hear what's been going on."

"Rose . . ." Gandy said sternly, lowering his chin as though he were aiming lightning bolts with his eyes.

Rose's eyes grew suddenly as sharp as her father's. Just as suddenly, the sharpness left her gaze, and she said with studied meekness, "Yes, Papa."

When Rose had dismissed herself to the loft, she and Ebeneezer Coleridge fairly screwing with their eyes as the space between them widened, Solomon Gandy leaned over the table and glanced at each of the three newcomers in turn.

"As we all know, Deputy Long is here to help us with the problem the Good Lord has found fit to test us with. My question to you, Deputy, is how do you propose to do that?"

"Indeed," said Ebeneezer Coleridge, who'd removed his hat and was obsessively smoothing a rooster tail. "I hope you have more men on the way, for you're certainly going to need them. Why, one man cannot stop the Hawk Haughton Bunch from harassing our gold shipments."

"I realize that," Longarm said. "Believe me, I'd have the entire frontier cavalry here if Uncle Sam could spare them from various troubles elsewhere."

The express agent, Boyd Spandhauer, blinked with disbelief. "You mean, you really are here *alone*?"

"I told you he was comin' alone!" rumbled Solomon Gandy like Moses on a mountaintop.

Yoakum said with consternated chagrin, "Yes, but I couldn't quite believe the U.S. marshal's office would really send only one man to try to solve such a dire problem."

When Longarm had told them that he'd been sent to track the devils to their lair, then call for more firepower as needed, Gandy cleared his throat and turned that dark gaze on Longarm, who suddenly felt sorrier for Rose than he had before. "Problem is," Gandy said, "I got another gold shipment headin' out day after tomorrow. They'll most likely try to hit it, because there's rumors floatin' around that they're gettin' ready to pull out of the country, head to Mexico."

"Why don't you postpone it for a week or two, give me time to nose around?"

"I got federal contracts that says I gotta keep gold moving to the mint in Denver City. Besides, I need cash. I got overhead, men to pay—miners, ore haulers, wood haulers, men who work the stamping mill, the smelter, and the foundry. They get paid weekly. If I'm shut down for just one day, I'd have to borrow money to pay those men."

"We can't afford another robbery, Deputy Long," said Yoakum. "Have you any idea how much money Mr. Gandy and the rail line have lost in the past year?"

"I'd guess a couple hundred thousand."

The one-eyed secretary who looked like a gunslinger—one whom Longarm had crossed paths with somewhere before—was consulting a leather-bound notepad, running a pencil down the page. "Seven hundred and sixty-seven thousand dollars to be exact."

"The shipments are insured, aren't they?"

"Of course," said Spandhauer. "The freight company pays in full to the mine whatever gets stolen during shipping. But the freight company is already badly overtaxed. One more robbery could very well ruin us." Spandhauer folded his soft, white hands on the table, a pinky ring annoyingly reflecting window light at Longarm. "And you see, Mr. Gandy is half-owner of the freight company."

Gandy slammed a fist on the table. "In other words, I'm out half of what they're out! And if the freight line goes under, I'll have to figure out my own way of shipping my gold. That's gonna cost money, time, and manpower."

Longarm dug a three-for-a-nickel cheroot from his coat pocket. "Gold camps ain't exactly howlin' for lack of gunslicks. Fight their gunslicks with your own. Hire more guards."

"Done that," Gandy said. "I put out feelers along the Devil's Trail, may the Lord have patience and understanding. Who comes callin' but that ole killer Earl Fox and his brother-in-law Matt Hardy and Pistol Pete Monroe from up Idaho way? Five more ringtail roarers came day before yesterday, applied to the mine office, and I made 'em shoot targets for me. Signed up three. The three ain't fast, you understand, but they're good marksmen and they don't mind killin'. I figure I'm fightin' evil with evil, and the Lord will understand."

Longarm said, "That should help your odds." He cast his gaze at Spandhauer. "But that narrow-gauge creeping up and down those passes is an easy target. You best outfit the express car with quarter-inch steel plating. Steel plates on every wall including the ceiling. Put slits in the plates for rifle barrels, so your gunslicks can return fire when they're attacked."

Spandhauer frowned. "The gold is secured in two locked steel boxes, Marshal Long. How much more . . . ?"

Gandy looked at the express agent. "Couldn't hurt. Get on it, Boyd."

"But we have only two days, Sol."

"Get on it," Gandy repeated, louder. "Get every smithy in Lulu City workin' on those plates, and don't let 'em quit till they're done!"

Spandhauer started to rise, but Longarm stopped him with another question. "Who all knows when each gold shipment is scheduled to leave Lulu City?"

"Until four hours before the gold's due to ship, only the four of us," said Yoakum as he doodled on his pad. "Then the bullion man at the mine needs to be informed. His men haul the strongboxes by mule to the train station. Then, and only then, do the conductors and engineers learn about it."

"Then how in Christ's name does the gang know when to get a holdup organized?" Longarm said to no one in particular.

A hushed silence descended like sudden rain. Gandy lifted his chin and drew air through his nose. "Deputy Long, I'll thank you not to take the Lord's name in vein."

Feeling like a chastised altar boy, Longarm apologized.

"*This* one we've discussed," young Coleridge said snootily. "They must have one or two men watching constantly from one of the many ridges between here and Colorado Springs. The train can't move very fast through those gorges, so it wouldn't take them long at all to gather at a prearranged spot when they've identified the express car."

Longarm said, "How do they know the gold's on the car?"

"We figure they probably have a man on every train heading down mountain," Yoakum said. "Anyone could see us loading the gold into the express car just before the train pulls out. We can't keep everything a secret. The Hawk Haughton man could signal to the men on the ridges in any number of ways. Maybe he waves a handkerchief out a window."

Longarm kicked his chair back, his legs out, and crossed his ankles. Puffing the cigar, he stuck his fingertips in his vest pockets. "Seems a might impractical for a gang that size to be holing up along the tracks. They know they're the most wanted men in this neck of the mountains."

Gandy said, "You think someone at this table might be sellin' secrets to Hawk Haughton? Forget it. Ebeneezer here, due to marry my Rose next fall, stands to inherit my grubstake. There'd be no point in trying to steal it piece-meal now and split it with Hawk Haughton.

"Phil Yoakum comes recommended by none other than General William T. Sherman himself, to whom he was aide-de-camp for three years during and after the war. That missing eye and a couple of other injuries inflicted by Red Cloud's pagans got him mustered out of the army. He's a patriot, not a thief, and as trustworthy as I am."

After only a second's pause, Gandy turned to Spand-hauer. "Boyd here might try to get his hands on a couple bars of my gold, but one, there must be an easier way than getting it through such ringtails as the Hawk Haughton Bunch, and two, he knows I'd twist his head off with my own hands and mount it on my cabin door if I found him out!"

No one seemed to have much to say after that. So Long-arm plucked his cigar from his mouth, studied the coal, and said, "I'm gonna find me a bed and sleep on it. The Hawk Haughton problem, that is."

"You can stay here, Deputy," Gandy said, adding, "if you can watch your language."

Longarm grinned around his cheroot. "I better hightail

64

it for ole Gomorrah. Best place for a lout like me. Besides, I might uncover clues as to where the gang is holin' up. If not, I'll accompany the gold train day after tomorrow."

"Is that wise, Deputy?" asked Yoakum. "If you're held up, you won't be able to follow them without a horse."

"I said accompany," Longarm said. "Not ride in the express car. I'll be on horseback, scouting as far ahead as I can. If the train's held up, I'll try to help with a rifle from atop a ridge, or track the gang back to their hole." He glanced from man to man. "Can anyone suggest sleeping quarters?"

"Brothel or dyed-in-the wool bunking quarters?" asked Gandy distastefully.

"They separate 'em in this camp?"

"I suggest the London. You'll sleep alone, however. The woman who runs the place, the Widow McBryde, is God-fearin' like myself, though for the life of me I don't see how she lives amongst all those heathens, and more comin' daily."

"Well, they must be comin' to either work for you directly or to support your miners," Longarm said, unable to hold his tongue. He'd never been able to keep his heat around temperamental old hypocrites like Gandy. "Yours is the only large workings in these parts, isn't it?"

Gandy just stared at him over the bowl of his pipe. "If you'd like a ride down to Gomorrah, Deputy Long, I'm sure Mr. Coleridge or Mr. Yoakum would oblige you."

Rising and donning his hat, Longarm said he could use the walk to start getting the lay of the land.

When he'd bidden good day to the four men in the kitchen and had turned to the door, he stopped suddenly. "Say, what about the local law? I heard deputies had been killed in the holdups."

Coleridge snorted while Gandy shook his head. "Hulbert Hooley. Don't expect any help from him. He was a drunkard before Hawk Haughton started striking my shipments, and he's only gotten worse. He's an old prospector who took the job when the town was still only three cabins and a handful of test holes."

"He's in over his head," Spandhauer agreed as he rose from the table and donned his beaver hat. Jerking his frock coat down over his paunch, he added, "Especially now that we got parasites on the gold trail."

Longarm squinted one eye. "Chew that up finer for me. It was a long train ride and I'm slow to cipher."

Gandy answered for the mine manager, who donned his riding gloves and left.

"There's a mother lode of gold—*my* gold—somewhere in these mountains. Wherever Hawk Haughton's stowed it. Half the mooncalfs with cap-and-ball pistols and Spring-field rifles are out beatin' the brush for it. Those too lazy to do any *real* work for a livin'."

"Three men have already disappeared," Yoakum said, then tipped back his coffee cup. "Got likkered up, loaded themselves for bear, and promptly never came home."

"Well, that oughta teach the others a lesson," Longarm said.

"Some," Gandy allowed, his voice taut with barely con-tained fury. "Some still think they're going to find their El Dorados and *somehow* get it away from that gang of cut-throats without getting their throats cut." He shook his big head, his leathery face red behind his perpetual tan. "When it rains, it pours."

Longarm allowed that was right, then nodded a final good-bye and walked outside. Closing the door behind him, he saw Spandhauer's wagon drifting off over the hill's shoulder, dust sifting behind the high red wheels. The air over the western hogbacks owned a purplish haze from Gandy's smelter. The hammering blows of the stampers shook the ground beneath Longarm's boots.

He adjusted his cartridge belt on his lean hips, stepped off the porch, and started down the trail. A wooden rasp sounded behind him, and he turned to see Rose stick her head out of an upstairs window.

"I'll be seeing you again, I hope, Custis!"

Longarm's face warmed. He wasn't sure what to say to that—the girl was due to be married, for Christ's sake!—so he merely pinched his hat brim to her, then turned, stuck his hands in his pockets, and headed off down the trail. He was glad when he heard the window rasp close behind him, and quickly scoured Miss Rose Gandy from his mind.

Wise men did not repeat their sins.

In Lulu City, he'd have a good, long nap, a shot of Maryland rye, and a bloody steak, then take a tour of the camp. He'd have bet silver cartwheels to navy beans that members of the gang were hanging around Lulu City. Hardcases like those couldn't go long without cards, liquor, and women. . . .

He'd taken a shortcut down the incline, bushwhacking through the buckbrush and wild mahogany and receding snowdrifts, when the thunder of galloping hooves rose in the west. Longarm turned, his right hand automatically going to the walnut grips of his double-action .44.

He kept the Colt in its holster, however. The horsemen were fast approaching, the ground vibrating beneath Longarm's low-heeled cavalry boots. There were too many riders—five or six—to fight off with only his Colt and double derringer, and with no cover within diving distance.

"Well, who do we have here?" he muttered to himself as the riders skidded their sweaty mounts to a collective halt before him, spraying dust over his boots.

Their faces were covered with burlap sacks, spaces for the eyes and mouths cut out. All five were aiming old-model carbines at him.

Longarm couldn't believe his luck would have soured this bad, but the chill hopscotching his spine told him he was about to meet the Hawk Haughton Gang sooner than expected—and, most likely, his Maker.

Chapter 8

Longarm removed his hand from the walnut grips of his
Colt as the five masked riders surrounded him. "Wrong
time of the year for Halloween," he said, glancing at the
yawning rifle bores aimed at his head and chest. "So let me
guess. A masquerade ball?"

The riders didn't say anything, just sat their saddles
breathing through the mouth holes in their burlap masks.

"No need to be so shy, boys. You're all wearin' masks. I
reckon I'm the odd man out!"

"Shut up, lawman," said the man atop a speckle-gray
mare. He wore a denim coat and patched breeches. On his
hip was an old Dance Brothers dragoon pistol. The carbine
aimed at Longarm was a seven-shot Spencer. "You the one
they sent up from Denver?"

"I believe you have the advantage. Who might you fel-
las be?"

"None of your business."

The man with the antique pistol glanced at a man behind Longarm. As Longarm turned, a rope loop shot out
from a hazel-eyed hombre atop a hammer-headed blue
roan. Longarm ducked too late. The loop dropped over his
head and shoulders.

As he raised his arms and moved to fling away the loop, the rope jerked taut, squeezing the air from his lungs and cutting into his ribs.

"Let's take this badge-toter for a ride, boys!" yelled the man atop the blue roan, stabbing the horse with his spurs.

Longarm spread his feet, setting himself and grabbing the rope with both hands. He'd be damned if he'd let them drag him. He'd jerk the roper off his damn horse and stamp the man to death.

The thought had no sooner rifled through his brain than he was jerked off his heels so abruptly that he nearly lost his boots. His hat flying back behind him, he hit the ground hard on his left shoulder, an excruciating pain shooting up and down his arm and into his chest. What little air that was left in his lungs blasted out with a guttural *"Fuck!"*

He was pulled forward so quickly and with such brain-numbing speed that all he could do was grit his teeth and hold the rope, keeping his head above the ground so he didn't break his neck on a rock or a shrub.

"Fuckin' Goddamn cocksuckin' sonso'bitches!" he spat as the blue roan kicked up dust before him, Longarm's long body fishtailing through the sage, hops, and needle-brush as he leaned this way and that, avoiding the larger rocks and brush clumps and cedars driving toward him.

The four other riders galloped to both sides, whooping and hollering, their horses snorting, bridle chains jangling. Longarm was so disoriented that he wasn't sure which direction they were headed, but he could tell they were angling down the ridge, probably away from Lulu City.

One man removed his hat to slap his swaybacked horse's rump, showing a shock of long, dark-red hair trailing out the bottom of his mask. Longarm would live through this one way or the other, and he'd find that son of a bitch and blow his eyes out the back of his head.

But not before the man told him who the others were . . .

As they crossed a sandy flat, Longarm reached down for

his pistol, but slapped only leather. The .44 must have fallen out of its holster.

Snapping another curse, Longarm returned his right hand to the rope and squinted against the dust, brush, and rocks blurring past him, the blue roan's tail waving before him, as if to mock him, above and between the horse's lunging rear legs.

Sand blasted his face, plugging his nose and obscuring his vision.

Just as he shot over a juniper shrub, the blue roan skidded to a stop thirty feet ahead, and then the ground stopped sliding beneath him. The world spun, but his elbows and knees were firmly planted.

His head swimming, he looked up and around through the waving dust.

The roan trotted toward him, the rider dismounting, the rope coil in his hands. As the other riders gathered around Longarm, the rider of the blue roan—a short gent with a paunch bulging his blue denim work shirt—squatted beside the lawman. He jerked the rope up over Longarm's shoulders and away from his head, and coiled it.

"If I was you, lawman," he said snidely, "I'd hop the next train home. You stay around here, messin' in stuff that ain't none of the gov'ment's business, we're gonna drag you all the way to Utah."

Longarm looked into the man's gray-blue eyes, both eyes bloodshot as though from too much drink the night before. The man nodded as if to send his message home, looked at the others, laughed, then walked back to his horse. Looping the lariat over the saddle horn, he swung into the leather and faced the others.

"Let's go, boys!"

Beckoning, he swung the roan around, put the steel to it, and galloped westward through the brush and boulders.

The others turned their mounts in the same direction, one hacking a spit wad at Longarm, then chuckling and spurring his horse after the others. He'd ridden only ten yards, however, when his horse lurched right of a prickly pear clump.

The man screamed and tumbled down his right stirrup fender, hit the ground, and rolled. His horse ran twenty more yards, stopped, and half-turned, its reins hanging. Groaning and holding his right side, the rider cursed the horse, gained his feet, hobbled forward, and heaved himself into the leather.

"Rabbit-hearted son of a bitch!" he yelled at the horse, assaulting the dun with his spurs and galloping into the sifting dust of the others.

Longarm groaned and lowered his head to the gravel, catching his wind.

He moved his arms and legs. He ached like Job, but nothing seemed broken. His elbows and knees burned, and when he finally found the strength to sit up, he saw that the undersides of his coat sleeves were torn. So were the knees of his brown tweed britches, his balbriggans peeking through. He was caked in seeds, dust, and sand.

Looks like Billy Vail and Lemonade Lucy Hayes would finally get their way. Longarm would have to invest in new duds out of his own pocket.

The thoughts belied the anger searing him, churning the bile in his gut. Standing, he turned in the direction of the galloping horsemen, dust sifting over the wagon trail they'd followed westward into fir and pine woods.

Those boys were too down at the heels and under-armed to be the Hawk Haughton Bunch. No doubt a group of the very would-be gold scavengers he'd just been told about.

Still dizzy and fuming, he staggered up the slope, following his own scuffed trail, eyes searching the ground. He stopped when the sun winked off gun metal, then crouched to retrieve his double-action .44 half-hidden under a sage branch.

Rubbing dust from the revolver, he slid it into his holster, then strode quickly across the shoulder of the ridge toward Lulu City clumped in the valley a hundred yards beyond. He'd fetch his rifle, then rent a mount at a livery barn, track the sons of bitches that had just played drag-the-deputy, and throw them all in the hoosegow.

Halloween party over.

Or maybe he'd just shoot them.

Yeah, he'd shoot them. Give himself an early Christmas present.

Fifteen minutes later, Avery Winters reined his blue roan to halt at the brow of a hill, the sun angling through tall pines on either side of the trail. He removed his battered Stetson, plucked the feed sack from his head, and slapped it against his thigh, blowing dust.

He turned the roan quarterwise and looked behind as the other four riders checked their own mounts down, lifting their hats and removing their own sacks from their sweaty heads.

"Better hold onto your masks, boys. I got a feelin' we might need 'em again. That lawman's got him an ornery streak. I could tell right off."

"Looked pure ornery as a jackass on Thunder Ridge," said Todd Gallantly, reaching behind to stuff his own mask into his saddlebags. He shook out his long, red hair, sweat flying, then donned his funnel-brimmed hat. "Looked a mite piss-burned too. What if instead of hoppin' the next train back to Denver, he tries trackin' us down?"

"We'll shoot him," said Winters, gray-blue eyes flashing angrily. He was short but strongly built, with short, blond hair and a neck stout as an ore wagon's rear axle. "Now, suppose you lead the way to wherever you left Roberts and Bascom. The trails in these Goddamn mountains all look alike to me."

Earlier, Todd Gallantly had ridden back to the sawyers' camp he shared with Winters and several others. He, Blacky Roberts, and Skip Bascom had spent the previous night gambling in the Bonanza Hop House in Steamer Gulch, with three men they'd suspected were none other

72

than Hawk and Ephraim Haughton and one of their gang members.

When the game had folded and the three presumed outlaws rode into the night, the sawyers had followed until they'd lost the trail in the pitch-black canyons northwest of Lulu City.

The plan was for Roberts and Bascom to wait at the spot where they'd lost the trail. Meanwhile, Gallantly would retrieve the other four sawyers, so the entire group could sniff the gang's trail by daylight. However, Gallantly had arrived at the sawyers' camp south of Lulu City to find the other sawyers cutting up feed sacks with the intention of hoorawing the lawman they'd heard was arriving that morning at the Lulu City train depot.

What rotten luck—having a deputy U.S. marshal sashay into town just when the sawyers had finally gotten up their gumption to track and confiscate the stolen gold! They'd all agreed that chances like this didn't come around but once in a man's life. While they had no idea how they were going to dispose of Hawk Haughton's gang members *exactly*, they would pure-dee find a way, by God, and the devil take the hindmost!

With the federal suit out of the way, now they could continue on to the rendevous with Blacky Roberts and Skip Bascom—who'd no doubt gotten themselves good and lost in those canyons anyhow, and they'd have all gotten themselves juiced up again for nothing.

Todd Gallantly lifted his hat and grinned. "Follow me, boys . . . to El Dorado!"

As he put his swaybacked dun down the rocky hill and into the deep forest shadows below, the others followed suit. Avery Winters spat and turned his roan in beside the big, bulbous-nosed German, Nils Bauer, and grunted, "El Dorado, my ass. I don't trust Todd or them other two boys to track their own shadows, let alone Hawk Haughton."

"Yah," said Bauer, pulling back on his paint's reins as the shod hooves clattered on the rocky incline, a hand-carved pipe protruding from his big, horsey teeth. "But if dey did track dat bunch, we can spent our time fucking da brown-skinned girls instead of the woodcutting for pennies and piss water, yah?"

The German's guffaws echoed like thunder.

Winters and Bauer followed the other three sawyers through the deep, short canyon, then over a ridge and into another. The day was heating up, the sun hot in spite of the lingering spring chill and stubborn snowdrifts, when Gallantly stopped his horse on an ancient Indian trail hugging a hill shoulder still mounded with dirty spring snow sprinkled with yellow pine needles.

Winters drew his blue roan up beside the long-haired redhead, who'd produced a spyglass from his saddlebags and was snugging it up to his eyes, adjusting the focus.

"What is it?" Winters grumbled, impatient. "You see them?"

"I don't know what the hell they're doin'," said Gallantly, holding the glass to his right eye. "I see their fire, see *them*, but Blacky and Skip're just *sittin'* there."

Winters followed Gallantly's gaze into a wide ravine below the hill shoulder. Hogbacks of mossy stone slabs, cedars reaching from the cracks, lay on the ravine's far side. In the hollow between two such slabs, thin blue smoke curled. At the base of the smoke, two figures slumped around a stone ring.

"Let me see!"

Winters grabbed the spyglass away from Gallantly, snugged it to his own eye. When he'd adjusted the focus, he saw little more than what he'd seen without it—just a few more details, like the dented black coffeepot sitting in the fire, and the saddle one of the men was lying against, a red-and-gray saddle blanket draw up to his chest. The man lay on his side, legs curled, black boots and spurs protruding from the bottom of the blanket.

"What the fuck are they doin'?" Winters said to no one in particular. "Sleepin'?"

"I don't like it," Peach McGinnis said, sitting his cream gelding off Winters's right stirrup. "Don't like the smell of it."

Gallantly turned to Winters, his brown eyes fearful. "Go down and check it out, Avery. Signal us if all's clear."

Winters jerked an exasperated look at the redhead. "Why the hell should—" He stopped himself, snorted disgustedly, then slapped the spyglass against Gallantly's chest. "Never send a faggot to do a man's work."

With that, Winters put his horse down the ravine, letting the roan choose its way, lunging and blowing. At the bottom, he booted the mount into a trot and, riding as tall as he could in the saddle, and keeping one hand on the grips of his Dance Brothers dragoon, rode toward the mouth of the ravine formed by the two gray hogbacks.

Chapter 9

Winters stopped his horse at the ravine's mouth.

The horse nickered and tossed its head, jumpy. Winters stared into the ravine where, fifty feet back, between the two sloping rock walls, the two men reclined beside the fire.

Winters considered calling out to the men, but something held him back. Cursing under his breath, he dismounted, looped his reins over a small fir, shucked his old revolver, and began moving into the ravine.

He thumbed back the Dance's hammer, aimed the pistol out before him, swinging it from side to side with his gaze. It would be just his luck to get bushwhacked in here, like a bug in a bottle. Sweat dripped into his eyes and down his cheeks.

When he was twenty feet from the fire ring, he stopped again. He could see both men clearly from this angle, a thumb of overhanging rock falling back out of the way. The smell of scorched coffee tanged the air, but otherwise everything appeared fine.

Both men appeared to be sleeping, Roberts on Winters's side of the fire. Bascom, the rangy ex-Pony Express rider, was on the opposite side, sitting on a log, his back and head resting against the rock wall behind him, his wide-brimmed black hat tipped over his eyes. His arms were crossed on his chest, his legs crossed at the ankles.

Maybe they'd been so jumpy all night, they hadn't been able to sleep, Winters thought. Now that it was full light, they'd decided to catch a few winks while waiting for the other sawyers.

Winters stepped forward and kicked a rock.

Neither man moved. He couldn't tell if they were breathing. Goddamnit.

Finally, with an impatient chuff, the foreman marched up to the fire and stopped. "Blacky," he said. "Skip."

Nothing.

Winters took another gander around. Nothing but wisping smoke, ankle-high dormant brush, and rock. Farther up the ravine, a cottontail crouched at the base of a boulder, its ears flat, trying to blend in with the rock.

Winters's stomach tightened with annoyance. His heart thudded with apprehension.

He kicked Roberts's knee-high, lace-up boot sticking out of the blanket. "Blacky, Goddamnit, wake up!"

The man only jerked a little from the kick. His eyes remained closed beneath the floppy brim of his hat.

Again, Winters looked around. He felt as though someone were watching him, but maybe he was only sensing the other sawyers watching from the trail. To his right, the dying fire crackled and the coffeepot sizzled as moisture ran down its side and dropped into the glowing coals.

Winters leaned down, grabbed Blacky's arm, and rolled the man onto his back. He'd opened his mouth to say the man's name, but only a sharp inhalation sounded. Winters jerked back as if slapped, and stared down in horror.

Blacky's nose was gone, leaving a black, bloody hole. Blacky stared up sightlessly, his jaw hanging slack, mouth forming an O. Winters dropped his eyes to the blood-stained blanket, jerked it down with one hand quickly, as though it were hot.

The front of Blacky's deerskin tunic was caked with jelled blood and spotted with swarming flies. Winters had seen enough knife wounds to know Blacky had been stabbed.

His heart pounding and head swimming, Winters rose unsteadily, stumbled over to Skip Bascom. He jerked the man up by the front of his blue-plaid shirt.

Bascom's hat dropped down his chest, revealing the round, blue hole in Bascom's forehead, a short, thick stream of blood running down between his shaggy, gray-brown eyebrows. Waters gasped when he saw the two congealed blood masses where his ears had been.

He remembered seeing something odd in the fire ring, and he turned to the ring again now. Sure enough, what looked like three burned chunks of gristle right of the coffeepot were Blacky's nose and Skip's ears.

Waters swallowed quickly to keep from airing his paunch.

"What the hell's—?"

At the sound of the voice behind him, Winters wheeled with a grunt, swinging his old revolver around. He saw the four other woodcutters walking up to the rock ring, Todd Gallantly throwing up his hands as if to ward off a bullet. Holding the shot, Winters stumbled over his own feet and fell in the brush.

Gallantly shuttled his eyes from Winters to the two dead men lying on either side of the fire. His tone was taut and faintly accusing. "What the fuck's goin' on here, Avery?"

"What the fuck's it look like?" Avery said, his gaze jackrabbiting around the ravine as he swung his revolver from left to right and up and down. "Haughton drilled these boys deader'n hell!"

Gallantly and the four other men—bearded and dusty and sweat-soaked—stared down at their two fallen comrades, their eyes etched with horror. The big German swung around, his long, denim duster flying about his legs.

He tipped his head back to stare up the limestone hogback behind them.

"I tink vee best leaf dis place!"

Winters had gained his feet. He was beginning to step slowly backward toward the mouth of the ravine, staring down at the two dead men, when a voice said, "Just what in the hell do you boys think you're doin'?"

Winters's gaze leapt up the stone dike on his left, straight above Skip Bascom's earless body. A man stood there as if he'd materialized from thin air—a ghastly-looking creature in an ancient butternut-gray kepi, long bear coat, and faded Confederate cavalry slacks, a yellow stripe running down the outside of both legs. His spurred cavalry boots rose nearly to his knees.

The man must have been a good six and a half feet tall, but it was his face that attracted the brunt of Winters's attention.

It was a ghoulish death mask—round, flour-white, gray-whiskered, and grinning. Tiny blue eyes flashed grotesquely in the sunlight. The man appeared to be completely bald beneath his hat, and two large silver rings dangled from his ears.

His patch-bearded face was hacked and scarred. He wore a gold medallion around his neck, and two ivory-gripped forty-fives and a stag-butted bowie knife jutted up on his hips, through slits cut in his coat.

Winters's heart tumbled over and over as he realized he was facing none other than Hawk Haughton—the spitting image of how Todd, Skip, and Blacky had described one of the men they'd played cards with last night.

"Well, I'll be diddled!" shouted Todd Gallantly, reaching for his revolver but leaving the gun in its holster.

Haughton's own gloved hands were empty, but Gallantly must have sensed, like Winters, that if he slid that Schofield a quarter inch out of its holster, he'd be dead before he could fart.

"I asked you boys a question," Hawk Haughton said in a

petal-soft Southern drawl, hunkering down on his heels and regarding the men below him with utter perplexity. "What the fuck do you think you're doin'?"

Winters's vocal cords had ceased working. It appeared his companions were all experiencing the same trouble. In a shaggy line, they stood staring up at Hawk Haughton as though God himself were crouched on the ridge above them.

"Shit, what the hell you *think* they're doin', Hawk?" rose a voice behind Winters. "They're after our gold."

Winters and the other woodcutters half-turned.

On the opposite hogback stood at least a dozen men in all styles of ragged, dusty trail garb, each outfitted with a good twenty pounds of fighting iron and ammunition. One had stringy silver hair hanging to his waist and blowing in the breeze, and he wore two sawed-off shotguns in custom-styled holsters on his thighs. His face was pale and buzzardlike.

The man beside him was barely over five feet tall. He wore a shabby bowler hat, a butternut tunic, hide breeches cut off at the knees, and high-heeled boots little larger than a child's. A thick stogie protruded from his teeth. In his small right hand was a Winchester carbine with a skinning knife attached to the barrel, saberlike, with rawhide.

Winters closed his eyes as if to rid his mind of the bizarre visages lined out before him—each more outlandish than the other. But when he opened his eyes again, they were all still there—long-haired, snaggle-toothed, bearded, bloodstained fiends loosed from a sordid Southern hell.

Winters's ears were ringing so loudly, and his head was swimming so fast, that it took him a minute to realize that the men on the ridge behind him and Hawk Haughton on the ridge before him were laughing as though at the funniest private joke they'd ever heard.

They were guffawing and shaking their heads and slapping their thighs, bending over red-faced with mirth.

Just when Winters started to hear their laughs, whoops, and thigh slaps, they all suddenly fell silent.

"Kill 'em," Hawk Haughton said softly.

As the outlaw leader turned and walked away like a lord from his stables, Winters ripped his old Dance Brothers dragoon from its holster, and spun on his left heel.

But he didn't even get the old gun cocked before two forty-five slugs blew his heart out his back and into the brush beneath him.

Bruised, scraped, sore, and with one hell of a mad on, Longarm stomped into Lulu City and rented a blaze-faced dun from the proprietor of the Occidental Livery and Feed Barn.

When he'd retrieved his rifle and war bag from the train depot, and had snugged the rifle down in the rented saddle boot, he tipped his hat over his forehead and galloped west of town, picking up the trail of the five soon-to-be-sorry hombres who'd dragged him.

He'd tracked the gang for an hour when, on a low pass deep in the mountains northwest of Lulu City—the Thunderhead Range, he believed they were called—he reined the spirited dun to a sudden halt. He'd heard the screech of magpies and blackbirds for nearly ten minutes, and now he spied several birds circling in the air or milling about the rocks on the ravine's far side.

Frowning, he peered at the muddy trail beneath his horse's hooves. He continued forward until the tracks of the men he'd been following turned off the trail and into the ravine. He traced the pocked ravine floor to the mouth of a feeder ravine nestled between two limestone scarps.

The birds were swarming only a few yards beyond, the magpies' incessant, indignant screeches resounding like hammer blows against Longarm's bruised brain plate.

What was worse, however, was the fetid scent tinged with the smell of burning pine.

Longarm's eyes swept the ground. The men had dismounted here and walked into the ravine. After the men had left the horses, the five mounts seemed to have drifted off by ones and twos.

Longarm's own mount threw its head up, nickering, at the pungent breeze wafting from up canyon.

"A might whiffy on the lee side," Longarm agreed, wrinkling his nose and staring between the stone knobs. He could see little but flapping wings and jouncing, feathered bodies around what looked like the slumped forms of dead animals.

The lawman slipped out of the saddle, tied the dun to an ironwood shrub, then shucked his Winchester, ramming a fresh shell into the breech and off-cocking the hammer.

Holding the rifle straight up and down before him, he walked into the canyon, where he was promptly assaulted by the shrieks of several indignant hawks and magpies. Many of the birds lit from what they'd been feeding on, trailing several inches of bloody viscera, and winged up and over the stone hogbacks. Several fluttered only a few feet off to light in the dwarf pines and cedars to give Longarm hell from their precarious perches.

Longarm stopped several yards from what, when the birds had cleared, he saw was a fire ring still sending up a few wisps of white smoke from mounded ashes. As his eyes swept the blood-washed canyon, he clenched his gut to keep from jettisoning the breakfast he'd consumed at the Gandy cabin.

Those weren't dead animals. They were dead men.

The birds hadn't been working on them long enough to make the mess he saw before him. Walking up to one of the bodies, he saw that the ears and nose had been sliced off with a sharp knife. The odor was caused by said ears and nose—along with many others—having been tossed into the fire.

Walking amongst the seven defaced bodies, clutching a handkerchief to his nose and mouth, he found the man with the long red hair. He'd been shot six times in the chest, face, neck, and both legs. His eyes stared up at Longarm, still etched with the horror he must have felt when the first of the bullets had cut into him.

His nose and ears had been cut off after he was already dead. Apparently, it was a message to those who'd find him and his compatriots.

And that message was what? the lawman asked himself when he'd walked back to the mouth of the ravine, all antipathy toward the five who'd dragged him having suddenly evaporated. He dropped to one knee and, staring back the way he'd just walked through the blood-painted brush, lowered the handkerchief from his face.

"Don't come any farther," he said aloud, answering his own question as the ravens, crows, hawks, and magpies once again descended upon their carrion. He looked around at the hogbacks and at the shallow ravine behind him.

His heart thumped anxiously.

Obviously, the seven dead men had been tracked by Hawk Haughton right into an ambush. Not that long ago either. Haughton and his bunch were probably within a couple of miles. If Longarm could find their trail and follow them back to their lair, he could wire Billy and have reinforcements headed toward Lulu City by this time tomorrow.

And hell, Haughton wouldn't be expecting anyone to follow him now—not after leaving this mess on his trail for any others with similar ideas.

For others with more smarts than Longarm, that is.

He began scouring the area for the killers' sign, quickly finding their cartridge casings atop the southern stone hogback. After that, it wasn't hard tracking the men back to where their horses had been tied in a shallow canyon up the ravine from where the dead men lay.

He retrieved the dun and followed the trail of at least a dozen horseback riders for an hour before the boom of a heavy rifle broke the breezy silence. Fortunately, Longarm had just lowered his head to ride beneath a long-hanging pine branch, and the big-caliber slug hammered a rock wall behind him.

Unfortunately, however, the dun reared with a scream.

And before Longarm could shuck his own rifle, he was rolling backward off the dun's left hip. At the same time, out of the corner of his left eye, he glimpsed a man walking out onto a pinnacle of mottled black rock straight above.

Long, silver hair blew around the man's shoulders as he extended a sawed-off shotgun in each hand.

Chapter 10

As the screaming dun lunged out from under Longarm, hooves thundering, Longarm hit the ground on his chest and belly.

He'd spied the long-haired ranny with the brace of sawed-off gut-shredders, however. Instead of lying there wondering how hurt he was, he instinctively threw himself up and left, into the shadow of the pinnacle.

He couldn't have made a better decision. He'd no sooner hit the ground at the base of the pitted monolith than one of the shotguns roared from above, blasting up a hunk of gravel and pine needles between the two oval gouges Longarm's elbows had carved in the ground.

Longarm clawed his .44-40 from its cross-draw holster and thumbed back the hammer as he pressed his left shoulder to the rock. He looked up, but couldn't see the bushwhacker from this angle—only the man's long, slender, hatted silhouette angling on the sunlit downslope to Longarm's right.

The man's shadow shrunk, as though he'd dropped to one knee, no doubt trying to get another bead on Longarm.

Longarm spat pine needles from his lips and took two

steps out away from the knob. "I'm right here, you bush-whackin' son of a bitch!"

Longarm threw his arm back against the rock as another blast assaulted his eardrums. Two barrels of double-ought buckshot blew a crater in the earth, at least a quarter of one wad peppering his right shoulder, chewing through his frock and burning like acid.

Ignoring the pain, he again threw himself out from the base of the rock, extending his cocked .44 at the peak. The long-haired bastard stared down at him, both shotguns smoking in his hands. His jaw dropped, and just as he began throwing himself back from the edge of the peak, Longarm triggered two quick shots.

"*Unghh!*" the man screamed.

He jerked straight back, hit a thumb of rock behind him, dropped to his knees, and rolled over the peak's edge. Longarm leaped right as the man hit the ground with a thud, blowing leaves, dust, and needles. He still held one of the shotguns in his right hand. The second fell behind him, hitting the man on his back with a dull whack.

"There you go, you son of a bitch," Longarm muttered as, wincing against the pain in his shoulder and upper arm, he turned to sweep the slope with his eyes.

Could this hombre have been the only one out here, covering the asses of the rest of the gang?

As if to answer his question, hoof falls rose in the distance, growing louder as a single rider approached from one of the distant ravines creasing the apron-pleated slope. Longarm squeezed the Colt in his right hand, glanced around for his horse and rifle. Nowhere in sight.

Silently, he cursed. He'd sure like to have that long gun. . . .

He glanced down at the dead man. The hoof falls grew louder, though the rider was down in a distant cut. Longarm holstered his Colt and dropped to his knees. He whipped off his own frock, wincing as the buckshot bit sharply, and tossed it aside, then wrestled the dead man out of his long, black duster.

When he'd donned the duster and the man's high, steeple-crowned hat, he grabbed both shotguns, broke them each open in turn, and filled all four barrels with the wads he discovered in the dead man's coat pockets.

He'd just snapped the second gut-shredder back together when the rider's head rose from a cut. The horse's head followed, and then horse and rider were bearing down on him, the man's long, frizzy, black hair bouncing on his shoulders, silver eyetooth glinting below his mustache-mantled upper lip. He wore two pistols in shoulder holsters behind the double, brass-filled bandoliers crossing his chest. With his right hand, he clutched a Winchester Yellowboy repeater by the breech.

Longarm began walking toward him, holding both shotguns down low at his sides, the rabbit-eared hammers pulled back and locked. He held his head down, half his face hidden by the dead man's hat brim, and strode deliberately toward the rider.

He needed to get close, within fifteen feet, to take the man with the shotguns.

As he walked, he pricked his ears for the sound of other approaching gang members, hearing only the single set of thudding hooves. Maybe these two men were the only flankers, and the rest had ridden on to their lair. If not, the gods were about to piss all over Longarm.

Thirty yards away, the black-haired man hauled back on the reins, turned the speckled-butted dun sideways. "Jingo, what was the shootin'?"

The deputy shook his head and swung one of the shotguns out to point behind him.

"Now who's trailin' us, Goddamnit?"

Longarm shrugged and kept walking, keeping his eyes on the ground but watching the black-haired rider in the upper periphery of his vision. The man stared at him, eyes slitted as he sat his saddle tensely.

Suddenly, he snapped up the Yellowboy. "Hold it!"

Ten yards away from the man, Longarm brought up one of the shotguns, aimed it straight out in his right hand, and triggered the right barrel.

Ka-booom!

The blast echoed around the rocky scarps and the pines. Harried wings fluttered below.

The black-haired gent triggered the Yellowboy into the ground. Then, dropping the rifle, he rose up tight in his saddle, slapping both hands to the bloody hole in his belly. At the same time, the fiddle-footing horse reared, giving a shrill whinny and flinging the rider out of the saddle. In seconds, it had disappeared downslope, the thuds of its shoes fading with distance.

Longarm walked over to the black-haired man writhing in the dead leaves and pine needles. He'd pushed himself onto his knees, hands still clutching his belly, but kept his forehead pressed to the ground.

He struggled, moving his knees and grunting. The leaves beneath him were soaked in liver-colored blood.

Longarm kicked the man onto his back. The man cursed and pinched his eyes closed, grinding his teeth and miserably lifting one leg, then the other.

"Cocksucker!" he spat at the lawman staring down at him.

Longarm extended the smoking shotgun, aiming the left barrel at the black-haired gent's left eye. "If you tell me where ole Hawk Haughton has stashed the gold, I'll find you a sawbones."

The man relaxed, lowering one knee and letting the other one turn inward. He swallowed and, breathing hard but with a resignation moving into his eyes, scowled up at Longarm. "Fuck . . . you . . ."

His nose wrinkled. Then he heaved a long sigh and turned his head to the right. His eyebrows half-lowered, and his chest stopped moving. An eye-watering stench rose as he evacuated his bowels.

Longarm turned away, looking around for any more gang members as he growled, "Same to you, pal."

It took the lawman an hour, hoofing it around the cuts and washes at the bottom of the slope, to find his rented dun calmly foraging thimbleberry leaves along a half-frozen creek. When he'd bathed his buckshot-peppered arm and shoulder in the chill water, he mounted up and headed back to town.

He'd have liked nothing better than to continue sniffing along the Hawk Haughton Gang's fresh trail, to follow the cutthroat demons to their very doorstep, but he had to get the buckshot plucked from his hide before he bled as dry as a two-day-dead hog.

"Any sawbones in this here burg?" he asked the livery owner when he'd returned the dun to the barn.

The liveryman was more interested in the condition of his steamy horse than Longarm, whose upper left coat was caked with dry blood. "We had one, but his horse ran his buggy off a cliff last week. Got spooked by a dynamite blast in the mountains. There's a Chinee over to the laundry that does some wound-sewing and bone-setting, but he don't speak a lick of English and I heard tell he crippled an Irishman a few months back. You might try the Widow McBryde over to the London Hotel. She learned some doctorin' from her father, a bona fide sawbones back East. Watch your tongue, though. She don't cotton to blue language or whiskey breath."

Longarm told the liveryman about the men Haughton had ambushed in case anyone wanted to fetch what was left of their remains. The liveryman only scoffed at the would-be posse's foolishness, and picked up the lathered dun's left rear hoof. "Say, where'd you take this gelding anyways? Half the damn nails in its shoes are loose!"

Longarm didn't respond as he pushed through the small front door and out into the street. He waited for three fast-hauling wood wagons drawn by snorting, gargantuan mules, their heavy wheels throwing mud against the board-walks and buildings on the north side of the street, then set his hat for the ornate, two-story hotel at the west end of town.

He crossed the front porch and stopped to read the hand-lettered plaque right of the front door. "Please knock before entering. Only gentlemen and ladies need apply for rooms." Another sign demanded that mud be scraped from shoes.

Longarm snorted. Apply for rooms in a mining camp? The Widow McBryde must be crazier than a tree full of owls.

He knocked on the door. He could hear the hum of voices inside, but it was a good two minutes before the door swung open to reveal a bizarre-looking little man in a checked bow tie and with longish but carefully combed and pomaded hair. He was the size of a twelve-year-old boy, but his clean-shaven, pitted, hidelike face appeared to be that of a man in his hard-earned fifties.

His voice was high-pitched, tentative, his skeptical eyes taking Longarm's measure. "Help you?"

"I was told a Mrs. McBryde did some doctorin'," Long-arm said, looking over the gent's shabby, brown bowler into a shadowy antechamber where an oak desk was set be-neath a staircase. "My shoulder needs tendin'. I could do it myself if I had a pincers and an arm growin' out of my spine, but . . . Is she around—Mrs. McBryde?"

Footsteps sounded in the antechamber's shadows and, drawing the door wide, the little gent turned to a woman carrying a silver coffee service and six china cups. In a room to Longarm's left, men laughed. Cigar smoke wafted beneath the gut-prodding aromas of fresh-baked pastries.

"Ma McBryde, there's a gent here whose arm needs tendin'."

The woman was headed for a doorway on the left side of the hall. Stopping, she turned toward the light filtering into the room around Longarm, and the deputy's breath caught in his throat.

The woman standing before him resembled no "Ma" he'd ever seen before. High-busted and wasp-waisted, she wore her jet-black hair in a delicious, semiloose cloud atop her regal head. Wide red lips stretched as her brown eyes, dancing in the late-afternoon light, flickered across Longarm's broad frame.

Her skin, he noticed, was like polished ivory. The hands on the coffee service were long and fine, the nails carefully filed—the hands of a queen, or at least a railroad heiress.

And he'd never known a "Ma" as young as this woman either. She couldn't have been a day over thirty.

"Are you drunk, sir?" the woman asked casually, as if she were merely inquiring the time.

Longarm's face warmed. He removed his hat as he quickly considered his condition. She was the type of woman—overly civilized in spite of her kiss-demanding lips and loin-warming bosom—who could make you feel sheepish when you had nothing to feel sheepish about. "No, ma'am. It's still a little early for me."

"Have you been fighting?"

"Well, it depends on what you call fighting. I was salted with double-ought buck while attempting to arrest one of the Hawk Haughton Gang."

Ma McBryde's black brows drew together over her wide, lustrous eyes. "You're the lawman . . . from Denver City?"

"That's right."

Her eyes reconsidered him. "Why didn't you say so? Where were you hit?"

Longarm pointed to his left arm hanging stiff at his side.

Ma McBryde glanced at the little gent still holding the door open. "Upstairs, Sandy. Room Eight. Heat a bath and fetch bandages and towels, will you?"

Before either Sandy or Longarm could reply, she'd continued into the room where the men were conversing amidst the cigar smoke and pastry smells, her purple silk skirts rustling about her legs.

When Sandy had closed the door, Longarm said, "That's Ma McBryde?"

"That's her." Sandy slipped a key from the rack behind the desk and, limping deep on his left leg, made for the stairs. "Follow me."

"I sure wasn't expecting . . . *that*!" Longarm chuckled as he followed the little gent up the pine-plank steps between pine-paneled walls adorned with ornate bracket lamps and oil paintings of bucolic mountain scenes.

"Few do."

"What's with the 'Ma'?"

"Short for Maude. It's sort of a joke, I reckon, but Ma don't laugh about it, so I suggest you don't bring it up. I also suggest you don't get *likkered up* on the premises, Marshal. And don't even try sneakin' in one of the doxies from the saloons or whorehouses up the street. You could be General Tecumseh Sherman your ownself, and Ma would throw you out on your ear. Despite her looks, she's a good Christian woman, highest moral fiber. Her late husband was a reverend, you see, as was her father and even her *grand*father."

Sandy opened Room Eight and stepped inside the small, clean room with a brass bed, washstand, and charcoal brazier. The single window, framed by red curtains, looked out over Main Street.

"Go ahead and strip," ordered Sandy. "I'll bring water and a tub. Ma'll be up directly." He turned to leave, swinging the door closed behind him. He stopped, turned back. "Oh, and don't worry about Ma seein' you naked. She's seen half the men in this camp in their birthday suits, and she's never batted an eyelash."

Sandy went out and closed the door.

Chapter 11

"I have to tell you, Miss McBryde—"

"Mrs. McBryde."

"*Mrs.* McBryde." Sitting naked in the copper tub, Longarm winced as the beautiful, black-haired hotel owner plucked a lead pellet from the back of his left shoulder blade. "I do feel a tad on the self-conscious side, me bein' the only one in the room naked an' all."

Steam curled off the soapy water rising to just above his belly button.

"Well, I apologize for your self-consciousness, but performing such a task in such a fashion keeps blood from getting all over good bedding. And let me assure you that you will *remain* the only naked person in the room, Deputy Long." Wielding a steel tweezers, Mrs. McBryde dropped the sixth pellet she'd dug from Longarm's hide into the porcelain bowl sitting atop towels on the scroll-back chair beside her. She was sitting on a footstool beside Longarm, wearing a full-length, off-white, lace-edged apron over her dress.

"Now, let's get back to a more serious topic, shall we? Were you able to find out where the Hawk Haughton Gang is hiding out before they bushwhacked you?"

"No, I'm sorry to say. But I'm gonna head out there again as soon as I can."

"You won't be riding anywhere for a good twenty-four hours," Mrs. McBryde said, dropping another pellet into the bowl. "Some of these pellets went in deep. While I deem it best to leave the wounds open so they can breathe and dry out on their own, any rough-housing will open them up again, and you're liable to bleed to death."

"I reckon I'll hang around town tomorrow. See if I can sniff out any leads in the whorehouses or saloons." Longarm didn't add that he'd be scouting for the train day after tomorrow. The fewer people who knew about the Holy Smokes gold shipment, the better.

She plucked another pellet from his arm, then shuttled her gaze to his. "Deputy, would you quit staring at me, please?" She dropped the pellet into the bowl.

"Sorry," Longarm said. "I've just never known a woman as beautiful as you called Ma. I was expecting a wizened-up old crone with silver hair bunched up with rusty pins!"

She was fishing around in a another hole for another pellet, her lips so close to Longarm's shoulder that he could feel her warm breath against his skin. "Thank you for the compliment, but if you're flirting with me, you're wasting your time."

"Why's that?"

"I'm a Christian woman."

"Even Christian women have . . . uh . . . needs."

She shoved the pincers into the wound with a little more vigor than probably necessary. Longarm stretched his lips back from his teeth. "Ouch!"

"I don't have those needs." She dropped the pellet into the bowl and gave him a pointed glance. "I was married to a wonderful, God-fearing man, and I do not intend to fraternize with another until I find one just like the Reverend Roman Thomas McBryde III."

"My apologies," Longarm said, plucking a three-for-a-nickel cheroot from off the washstand to his right. He held it up to her and arched a brow, beseeching.

"If you must," she chuffed, probing another wound.

Longarm lit the cheroot, then sat smoking to dull the pain while she probed, prodded, and removed more lead. She ordered him to sit up on his knees so she could reach a couple of pellets that had penetrated farther down on his back.

When he'd done so, and when she'd plucked two stray pellets from down around his left kidney, she told him to sit back again while she cleaned and bandaged the wounds. Reaching for a long strip of cotton cloth on the chair, she glanced into the sudsy water.

"That's disgusting, Deputy!"

"What?"

"That."

Longarm followed her gaze into the water beneath his belly button. The round, dark-pink ball of his shaft protruded above the waterline, bobbing slightly with each pulse beat. It looked like a one-eyed frog peering around from a half-submerged log.

Longarm laughed with embarrassment. "Pardon me, Mrs. McBryde, but we males are a curious lot. We can be peppered with double-ought buck and still get aroused by the sight of a pretty woman. Take no offense. My thoughts are pure, but my dong has a will of its own!"

"I see that. Perhaps you should say a prayer. And just in case you're getting any depraved ideas, I need only scream once and I'd have Sandy up here with a double-barreled bird gun. I might be devout, Deputy Long, but I will not be trifled with."

Longarm's anger was causing his shaft to slip back beneath the water. "Ma'am, I'm offended by your offense! I've never forced myself on a woman in my life! Besides, you're the one who wanted me in my birthday suit!"

"Please keep your voice down, Deputy." She'd huffily

dried his back and was working on his chest, grunting with the effort, a few small clumps of her rich black hair falling down around her shoulders. Her face was red and radiant with indignation. "I have a reputation to uphold in this town. The men having coffee downstairs are respected businessmen, and I wouldn't want them to think anything untoward were happening up here."

She began wrapping strips of the cloth bandages around his back and chest. He smiled, watching her. Perspiration beaded her forehead and laid a sheen across her high, smooth cheekbones. He was pretty damn sure it wasn't caused by the steam from his bath.

"Don't worry, Mrs. McBryde." He raised the cigar to his lips, took a long puff. He held up his free arm so she could continue wrapping the cloth around his chest. "I'm in complete control." He loosed a perfect ring straight out over the water. "Are you?"

"Of course I am, Deputy Long," said Mrs. McBryde, an angry trill in her voice as she tied off the bandage. "I am always *quite* in control."

She stood, gathered the extra bandages and the implements she'd used to prod and cut, and turned to him haughtily. "Now, will there be anything else?"

"No, I reckon I'll probably take a long nap." Longarm stuck the cigar in his mouth, placed his hands on the sides of the copper tub, and lifted himself from the water. Standing, he turned to face her, rolling the cigar from one side of his mouth to the other.

She stood stiffly, facing him. Her eyes dropped to his waist and back up to his eyes. Her face had blanched. For a moment, he thought she would faint. Suddenly regaining her composure, she turned to the door, and went out.

Longarm removed the cigar from his mouth and looked down. His cock was as hard as the oak handle on a nine-pound hammer. It nodded at the door expectantly.

"Well, I'll be damned," he said, regarding the shaft as

though it were an incorrigible old dog. "You beat all, you know that?"

After two stiff belts from the Maryland rye he produced from his war bag, Longarm slept for a couple of hours. It was a deep, dreamless sleep unusual for a daytime nap. When he woke, darkness had fallen—the heavy, stygian dark of the high mountains that the stars could barely relieve in spite of their clearness and vigor. The lawman's head ached dully, and his bones and joints felt as though he'd been dragged over a rocky mountain shoulder and peppered with buckshot.

Appropriate, he figured, imbibing a couple more belts from his bottle.

Retrieving his spare duds rolled up in his war bag—denim trousers, navy flannel shirt, and cowhide vest—more appropriate garb for a mining camp and for trailing owlhoots through the long coulees—he dressed by lamplight. He winced and chuffed at the pain in his arm and shoulder, careful not to dislodge the thick pads Ma McBryde had positioned beneath the heavy cotton wrap.

Noting the mountain chill penetrating his room in spite of the sound walls around him, he donned his sheepskin coat and deerskin gloves, then set his hat on his head and went downstairs. Sandy sat on a stool behind the front desk, bathed in light from the bracket lamps, and while voices rose from the hotel's kitchen and parlor off the antechamber, Longarm saw no sign of Ma.

"How you feelin' this evenin', Marshal?" Sandy asked, looking up from his newspaper, a cuckoo clock ticking on the wall across from the desk.

"If I said fit as a fiddle, I'd risk adding a few inches to my nose, but I've felt worse." Longarm pinched his hat and headed for the door.

"Steppin' out, are ye?"

"Gonna mill around a little, get the lay of the camp."

"Ma has some vittles for you. She serves at six sharp every night, but since you were so down at the heels, she saved you a plate. She's in yonder, playin' euchre with Mrs. Benford, who lives here permanent."

"Thank Ma for me, will you, Sandy?" Longarm opened the door. "I'll get a bite while I'm making the rounds."

As Longarm stepped out, Sandy's voice stopped him. "Uh . . . Deputy Long . . ." The little gent seemed reluctant to continue, coughing dryly into his fist, then swiping a wing of greasy hair from an eye. "Ma also told me to inform you that our doors are locked at ten o'clock every evening. Since it's eight thirty now, you don't have a whole lot of time."

Longarm's chest tightened as he strode across the foyer, placed his gloved hands on the desk, and leaned forward. "Sandy, you tell your persnickety employer that I'm a big boy, and I'll stay out as late as I want. If she locks me out when I stroll back to the mattress sack around midnight or later, I'll arrest her for trifling with a lawman in pursuit of his duties."

He winked, nodded, strode to the open front door, and went out, hearing Sandy fatefully announce behind him, "I'll pass that along, sir. . . ."

Longarm strode eastward up Main Street, brightly lit with oil lamps and torches fixed to awning posts or poking up from sand-filled whiskey kegs. It was the middle of the week but, like most mining camps, Lulu City was hopping like a weekend. All the saloons and whorehouses were doing a brisk business amidst laughter, music, wafting wood smoke, and the mingling fetors of privies, street shit, doxie cribs, corn liquor, and tub-brewed beer.

Longarm stopped in the first hop house he saw—merely a tent filled with plain wooden tables and benches and a half-breed whore making the rounds in nothing but a pink chemise and fishnet in spite of the chill.

He asked the bartender if he'd spied any trail-worn, well-armed customers with Southern accents of late, and the burly gent with a livery-broom mustache stretched his lips back from his big teeth. "Hawk's boys, eh? No, sir, I ain't seen any of 'em in a couple of nights, though I heard they been playin' poker at some of the roadhouses outside town." His eyes swept Longarm's coat, looking for a badge. "You the federal?"

Puffing his cheroot and looking around the cramped, smoky room, Longarm nodded.

"Watch yourself," warned the barman, raising his voice above the catcalls of several burly miners at the far side of the tent. "Us bona fide businessmen are glad you're here, but for the love o' Jehovah, man, you're outgunned. There's already bets goin' up, and the odds aren't in your favor. We just ain't sure who's gonna git you first, Hawk Haughton or the men after Hawk Haughton's gold!"

The man laughed and slapped the bar planks with a big white hand.

Longarm offered a taut grin. "Thanks for the confidence."

"Anytime!" The barman laughed again and stepped away to refill a beer schooner a Russian mule skinner thrust toward him.

Longarm finished his beer and had two more in the Highgrader and Rocky Slope saloons respectively. He was about to hoof it off toward the jailhouse when he spied a man with a tin star on his vest arm-wrestling with a beefy, greasy gent dressed in miner's heavy denims and a red-plaid shirt rolled up his corded forearms. The glassy look in the sheriff's eyes, and the dozen or so beer and shot-glasses on the table before him, told Longarm he wouldn't get much out of the local law this evening. Probably *any* evening. So, answering the call of his aching and perforated hide for a bed, Longarm headed back to the west end of town, brass horns and fallen women blaring behind him.

He stopped on the London Hotel's dark front porch, and tried the doorknob. He grinned as the knob turned in his hand. Then he went inside, closed and locked the door behind him. By the cuckoo clock on the wall to his left, it was only eleven o'clock, but the London was quiet as a catacomb.

Either Ma or Sandy had left a lamp burning on the front desk. Longarm blew it out, then crossed the dark foyer to the stairs.

A latch clicked on his right. Instinctively grabbing his Colt from its cross-draw holster, he turned to see a door open, lamplight bleeding through the widening crack. A slender figure stepped out, silhouetted by the lamp the woman held in her hand.

"Who's there?"

"Longarm, Mrs. McBryde."

The woman stopped in the open doorway. She wore a white shift closed at her ample bosom, though it wasn't quite closed. There was about a three-inch gap between lapels. Her hair was down, and she looked very enticing and inviting, standing there with her breasts rising and falling sharply behind the thin cotton, the lamp guttering in her hand, making her eyes glow like copper.

Chapter 12

"Oh . . . it *is* you," said Mrs. McBryde. She shifted her weight as she stared at Longarm. "How'd it go, Deputy? Did you dig up any clues as to where the Hawk Haughton Gang might be hiding themselves?"

Longarm squinted. Her voice was thick. She stood uncertainly in her doorway, shifting her weight as if to keep from falling, as if half pie-eyed. But he couldn't smell anything on her breath. Behind her, the red-papered room shone dimly in the lamplight, shadows shifting to and fro across a four-poster bed with the sheets and quilts thrown back.

"All I learned was I'm headed for Boot Hill in a hay cart," Longarm said as he moved slowly toward her, shoving his gloves in a pocket and unbuttoning his coat with one hand. He stared down at her, watching her eyes move slowly up his chest to his face. The brown orbs were wide and soft, and her cheeks were flushed.

Longarm freed the last button and dropped his arms to his sides. "You gonna invite me in?"

"Of course not." Her voice was husky, and she swayed a little on her slippered feet.

"Then you best turn around and go back inside. Out

here, you're liable to catch a chill." He reached out and ran his index finger through the exposed valley between her breasts. Her skin was warm. "Since you seem to be naked beneath that shift."

She sucked a sharp breath and whispered, "How dare you!"

Longarm half-turned, wrapped his right arm around her. She tipped her head back and he closed his mouth down on hers.

She didn't kiss him back, but she didn't resist. He kissed her for a long time, then released her and stood looking down at her again, his eyes crinkled at the corners.

She was breathing hard, the high, proud breasts pushing at the shift, the nipples making two thimble-sized protrusions in the fabric. Longarm reached into the shift and cupped a breast in his hand, moving his thumb across the hard, pebbled nipple. She gave a little groan and threw her shoulders back, stared up at him with parted lips.

The nipple hardened even more at his touch.

Suddenly, she grabbed the fleece-lined lapels of his sheepskin coat and drew him brusquely into the room. She gave the door a light shove, and when the latch had clicked, he bent down and kissed her again.

She was more welcoming this time, rising up on her toes and mashing her lips against his, sticking her tongue in his mouth and groaning softly. She ran her hands up and down his chest, kneading his pectorals with the heels of her hands, probing with her fingers, igniting a fire deep in his loins.

Longarm pulled away. "Where's Sandy?"

"He sleeps in the barn. His preference. He likes to come in late from the hop houses. I ignore it, as it's difficult to find decent help in a mining camp."

"Mrs. Benford?"

"She takes sleeping powders." Ma McBryde stepped back and slid the shift off her shoulders, let it fall in a pile at her feet. "We're quite alone."

102

Longarm cupped both full, upturned globes in his hands, massaged them slowly at first, then harder. Her head fell back on her shoulders, and soft groans seeped up from her throat. Gooseflesh rose until her skin felt like the hide of a freshly plucked chicken, though hot and moist with perspiration. Her groans rose until they fairly echoed off the room's papered walls.

Finally, she stepped back, turned, and reclined gracefully on the bed. She rose up on her elbows, bent legs together, one foot atop the other, and invited him to join her with her glistening doe's eyes. Her heavy breasts flattened slightly, framed by her long, black hair, the nipples reaching out like small pink posts.

Longarm's throat went dry and his shaft throbbed painfully against his denims. His eyes ran up and down the woman's pale body bathed in flickering lamplight. He kicked out of his boots and unbuckled his cartridge belt.

Less than a minute later, he stood naked beside the bed, his iron-hard shaft jutting.

She crawled over to it, ran her right hand along it while cupping his balls with the right. She stuck her tongue out. While looking demurely up at Longarm, she ran the tip of her tongue along the shaft, the thrill reaching deep into the pit of the lawman's belly, sending little crickets of ecstacy leaping up his spine.

When he was close to climax, he stepped back, took a deep breath to quell his passion, then crawled onto the bed, kneeling between her legs. She spread her knees and lay, hands up by her shoulders, fingers curled toward the palms, staring up at him, beseeching him with her eyes.

Longarm dropped toward her, placing his hands on either side of hers, supported by his outstretched arms, and moved his hips toward hers, letting her guide him gently into her warm, moist center.

When he was all the way in, she wrapped her legs around his back, grinding her heels into his sides, tipping her head back and groaning through her open jaws.

103

Longarm slid nearly all the way in, then thrust forward—hard and deep. Again, he did the same thing, until he couldn't take it any longer—and neither could she, judging by the way she pounded her heels against his buttocks and dug her nails into his shoulders—and thrust more quickly, in and out, in and out, until he rammed his cock all the way into her, stopped, and let go.

She gave a shriek he was certain could be heard across Lulu City.

"Ma'am," he grunted, sagging toward her, sweat pasting their bellies together, "I do believe you haven't been entirely forthcoming with me . . . or with the good folks of Lulu City."

Panting, she swallowed and ran a brusque hand through his hair. "Why, Deputy Long, what on earth do you mean?"

He slid onto his side, cupped a firm, round breast in his hand, gently kissed the nipple. "You know what I mean, Ma. If that's your name."

"It's my name, Custis. *Can* I call you Custis?"

"I reckon it'd be plumb silly not to . . . under the current circumstances."

She sighed and ran her hand through his hair once more as he nibbled her nipples. "Oh, I'm a fallen woman, Custis! There, I finally admitted it to someone. You know how long I've kept the secret? It feels good to get it out." She looked down at him still working on her breasts. "But you won't tell a soul, will you? I'd lose respect and . . . and I'd be ruined."

Longarm lifted his head, resting his jaw on the flat of his hand. "Your secret's good with me. But only if you spill the beans. Not that it matters overmuch. There's plenty of women going by aliases out West. Plenty of men, for that matter. But you've aroused my curiosity."

"Let's just say, not to waste time with idle chatter as the night grows old, the Reverend found me singing in a Dodge City saloon when I was only sixteen—and made a respectable woman of me. Of course, what he was doing

104

there, he never explained. Suffice it to say, I became his wife and partner in the Lord Jesus Christ, and we traveled around together as Roman preached the Gospel.

"When he died from heart stroke"—she raised her hand to her mouth, covering a titter as she added—"I always did overly arouse the poor man. Anyway, when he died, I decided to carry on a respectable life, so I used the money he left to build this hotel. It's a lovely life, and I do dearly cherish it, but I tell you, Custis, sometimes I want nothing more than a man's cock between my legs!"

"I'm sure you can find someone around here who'd be more than willing to provide it."

"Yes, but these savages would spread it around that I'm a wanton woman, and my business would suffer. The pious town council—all of whom visit the tent brothels and grog huts regularly!—would drive me into the streets. I must keep up my reputation as the pious widow of the Reverend Roman McBryde lest I should work in the brothels myself and die of syphilis before I'm forty!"

"I see what you mean, Ma—"

"Zeena. Zeena Cromwell's my given name." She lifted her head, placed her open hand along his cheek, and tenderly kissed his lips. "You can call me Zeena, Custis. I'd like for you to. But so help me, if you ever speak of this night, or tell anyone my real name, I'll remove your balls with a rusty skinning knife and add them to my Tuesday tripe."

She kissed him gently once more, then pushed him onto his back and straddled him, brown eyes sparking like diamonds. "Now, what do you say we have us some *real* fun?"

Longarm was in no condition for the carnal high jinks that continued with animalistic fury until nearly two o'clock the next morning.

Before he and Ma McBryde were as spent as colts in their first thunderstorm, Zeena, as he preferred to call her now, had had to reclean and dress several of his buckshot wounds and rewrap the bandage around his chest and back.

105

Hot and sweaty and still breathing hard, Longarm kissed Zeena good night before blowing out her lamp and padding naked up to his room, carrying his clothes in his arms. He collapsed in his own bed, and didn't awaken until golden sunlight angled through his sashed window, tattooing his eyelids.

He lifted his head from his pillow, wincing at the aches and pains that his mattress dance with Zeena had aggravated, and lay listening to the ubiquitous stamp of the mine's mill and the thunder of men, stock, and wagons on the street below his room.

Nothing like waking up late in a burgeoning mining camp to make a man feel lazy . . .

When he'd taken a whore's bath and dressed in his trail duds, he went downstairs for breakfast in the London's small, elegant dining room. Zeena—or Ma—and a young Chinese girl were hustling food and coffee to several business types and a couple gamblers and four freighters when Longarm sat down.

Such was Zeena's showgirl's talent that she gave no indication of the sweat that she and Longarm had expelled in her room only a few hours ago. Without so much as a flush, she took his order, served his coffee, and set before him a heaping plate of scrambled eggs, bacon, ham, and buckwheat pancakes complemented by fresh-whipped butter, honey, and gooseberry preserves.

Longarm remained as cool as she, and by the time he left, no one in the room could have known he'd thrown the blocks to Ma McBryde not thirty feet from the dining room door—including the blue-haired crone sipping tea and nibbling buttered toast against the opposite wall, who kept casting busybody glances at him over her bone-china cup etched with pine cones.

Mrs. Benford, no doubt. Her sleeping powders had been hard at work last night; otherwise, she'd probably have had the town council burning him and Zeena at the proverbial stake about now.

At the livery barn, Longarm rented the same horse he'd rented the day before, and rode up to Solomon Gandy's cabin. He wasn't surprised to find the old prospector stretching a fresh cougar hide in his backyard. His business seemed to have outgrown him, and he was content to live the simple life of a mountain man and let his future son-in-law endure the headaches.

Longarm knew he could ride up to the mine and, toting a federal badge, take his own tour of the works. But having Gandy show him around would save time. The old man was agreeable, and saddled his own horse—a beefy grulla named King.

They followed the twisting wagon road to where three mine portals appeared above yellow slag heaps. At the base of the mountain, surrounded by a fortlike stockade, stood the mine offices, stamping mill, and the three warehouses holding the foundry, retort room, and vault.

"I beg forgiveness every day for the desecration of God's mountain, as this used to be a right lovely place, and quiet as the Kingdom of Heaven," Gandy said mournfully. "But a man must work, earn a living, feed his children. . . ."

Longarm didn't say anything, only wrinkled his nose at the stench from the smelter stacks and the ground-jarring rumble of the stamping mill.

"Oh, well," Gandy said, swaying in the saddle. "'His mercy endureth forever.'"

The Holy Smokes was like most mining operations Longarm had seen, only slightly larger and run with more of a frenzy, it seemed, with Ebeneezer Coleridge running the show in shirtsleeves. Gandy showed Longarm around, introducing him to the superintendent of the bullion storage area—a small room sealed in iron.

The superintendent, a little old man named Karl Steffan, clad in a striped shirt with a poet collar, a green eyeshade, and pince-nez spectacles, led Longarm and Gandy into the bullion room. He opened one of the two boxes due for transport the next day.

Fifteen gold bars winked up at Longarm, each stamped HS LU CTY, for Holy Smokes Mine, Lulu City.

"Mr. Steffan," Longarm said, running the first two fingers of his left hand over one of the bars, "if someone was to sell these bars, they'd first have to change the stamp, wouldn't they?"

Steffan nodded and raised his voice above the thunder of the steam works supplying power to the mine works and stamping mill, and the roar of the wood and ore wagons. "Couldn't sell 'em like that. Who'd buy 'em?"

Gandy towered over the little bullion room superintendent. "They'd have to melt 'em down somehow, and recast them to erase that stamp. No mint would buy a stamp it don't recognize."

Longarm's next question was as much to himself as anyone else. "Would they recast the bars somewhere around here? Or, if they're operating out of Mexico, would they haul it all south of the border and *then* do it?"

"Wouldn't be easy, haulin' that much gold all the way to Mexico," Steffan said, poking his gnarled fingers into his vest pockets. "The men and wagons and mules they'd need would make them pretty damn conspicuous."

"Of course," Gandy said, "it's been done before. And they're a brash lot . . . playin' cards between jobs right here in Lulu City!"

"But it'd be a mite easier if they could melt the gold down here, and sell it to, say, the same mint *you* were going to sell it to—the one in Denver."

"If they put a new stamp on it," Steffan said with a fateful shrug, "there would be no tracing it back here less'n they did some elaborate chemistry on it, and the mint don't do that to every load of bars that come in."

"Thanks, Mr. Steffan," Longarm said, shaking the superintendent's hand, then letting Gandy show him the way out of the building.

On the porch of the main office building, Longarm stopped to light a cheroot and gaze into the dust. Steam and the smelter stacks' purplish fog washed up against the high, rocky ridges and mine portals before him. Ore wagons threaded down the steep grades terraced with timber slash and house-sized boulders, appearing the size of june bugs from this distance, and cinnamon-colored with dust and grit.

The air smelled of wood smoke, smelter ash, steam, hub grease, and mule shit.

Longarm turned to Gandy, Ebeneezer Coleridge, and Coleridge's assistant, Phil Yoakum, stepping out of the office behind him. Coleridge held a coffee cup. A pencil was snugged behind his right ear. Yoakum was dressed like a cardsharp or gunslick in a suit and vest, though he wasn't wearing a gun—at least, not where anyone could see it.

"When's the shipment leaving tomorrow?" Longarm asked, wondering once more where he'd seen Yoakum before. Maybe nowhere. Could be he'd run into so many one-eyed bandits, he'd become suspicious of them all.

Gandy opened his mouth to speak, stopped, and glanced at Coleridge. The young superintendent shuttled his glance from Gandy to Yoakum, then back to his boss.

"Oh, come on, boys." Longarm removed the cheroot from his mouth, blowing smoke. "You think a federal lawman's gonna come up here and join the gang's he's being paid to hunt?"

Fooling with his gold watch chain, Yoakum narrowed his one good eye. "I reckon we're just habitually cautious, Deputy."

Coleridge said, "We intended to tell you when we alerted the other guards and Mr. Steffan. We'll be loading the gold onto the train at nine o'clock, with guards armed with shotguns."

"You still insist on scouting ahead?" Gandy asked when he and Longarm were back on their horses, heading for Gandy's cabin.

"I can't think of a better way to lock horns with Hawk Haughton, can you?"

"I reckon not, but you're only one man. You're liable to

get greased up and butter-fried. You've seen for yourself what ringtails they are."

"Ringtails are my business, Mr. Gandy."

"Well, I reckon it's your behind, Mr. Long."

When they reached Gandy's cabin, Rose stepped onto the front porch to invite Longarm for lunch. She smiled with a little too much vigor, thrusting her nubbin breasts out. Longarm politely declined, tipping his hat to the gal. He told Gandy he'd see him at the train station at nine the next morning, then booted his mount toward Lulu City.

"Chicken!" Rose called behind Longarm, when her father had taken his horse to the stable behind the cabin.

Longarm didn't look back at her, just threw out an arm in acknowledgment.

When it came to the daughters of pious men, you're damn right he was chicken. Besides, he had bigger fish to fry in Lulu City.

Chapter 13

On his short trek down the mountain to Lulu City, Longarm ran the entire gold-thieving situation through his mind
and came up with a question he wished he would have
asked Solomon Gandy or Ebeneezer Coleridge.

If the gang was melting down the gold bars, pouring the
gold into fresh molds with a phony stamp, where around
here could they be implementing such an operation? It
wasn't like you can recast gold anywhere. You had to have
a foundry.

Longarm continued pondering the question, wondering
if any old mine works remained in this neck of the
mountains—probably abandoned works the gang could
have taken over relatively easily. He decided that the best
man to answer such a question, along with a few others he
had in mind, was the local lawman.

When he'd returned the horse to the livery barn, he
strode to the jailhouse sitting midway up Main, sand-
wiched between a saloon and a harness shop. Directly
across the street was a tall, two-story structure painted
bright pink and bearing a shingle that read OCCIDENTAL SA-
LOON, BREWERY, AND PLEASURE PALACE. On the boardwalk before the place were three short, sunburned,

cloth-capped miners holding frothy beer schooners in their roast-sized fists.

All three stood behind a young redhead who was clad in only a light, cream wrapper and powder-blue corset in spite of the cool temperature. The men were inspecting her ass, which she proudly stuck out and pointed at, as if to convince the men hers was the finest ass they'd ever seen.

The men chuckled sheepishly, elbowing each other, shaking their heads, and conversing in French.

Allowing that the girl had a right fine-looking ass but no better than, say, Ma McBryde's, Longarm turned to the jailhouse's stout timber door.

He raised his right fist to knock, but stopped when he saw the note nailed to the door. "Inquire for Sheriff Hooley at Gold Cache" was scrawled in smudged ink on the back of the moisture-stained wanted dodger. Beneath the words was a long arrow pointing to Longarm's right.

Longarm walked that way and stopped before the saloon next door. Over the window left of the batwings, the words GOLD CACHE SALOON were etched in large, gold-leaf letters.

Longarm pushed inside, where seven miners, looking weary and dirty from a long shift breaking and hauling rock, were playing poker on the left side of the room, while a plump brunette sat atop the bar on the right side. The brunette's legs were bare beneath her over-the-knee pantaloons.

A thick wolf coat was draped over her shoulders, and a cigarette drooped from her lips. She was pretty in a hard way, with pudgy cheeks and a cleft chin, and big, brown eyes taking Longarm's measure with delight.

She kicked a bare boot, let it fall back against the bar. "Hi."

"Hi, there."

She blew a smoke plume past his face. "Wanna poke?"

Longarm doffed his hat, leaned down, and planted a kiss on her knee. Straightening, he said, "Young lady, you'd be one hell of a fine way to pass the lunch hour. Unfortunately, I'm here to see the sheriff on business."

The man flanking her behind the bar, and reaching up to set bottles on shelves above the back bar, said, "Ah, shit, now what?"

He turned toward Longarm, holding a whiskey bottle by the neck. He was bald, with gray hair on the sides of his head and a gray, carefully trimmed beard and mustache. His eyes were liquid blue.

As he turned full around, Longarm saw the five-pointed star, which appeared to have been cut from the lid of a fruit tin, peeking out from under his apron. The corners of his mouth turned down. Longarm didn't know how the man normally looked, but he seemed a tad paler than he had last night while swilling whiskey and playing poker.

"You're that federal they sent, ain't ya?" the local lawman inquired, though Longarm wasn't wearing his badge. Apparently, the camp had been expecting him, and word of his arrival had spread like smelter soot.

"That's right." Longarm jerked a thumb over his shoulder, indicating the jailhouse next door. "You, uh . . . ?"

"I own the saloon too. Used to have a couple of deputies manning the hoosegow, but not no more. Not after Hawk Haughton started preyin' on the gold shipments. Gandy used my deputies to guard the express car, you see? Cheap old bastard. Well, they're dead now, and I can't get no one to replace 'em."

"Why's that?"

"Shit, *now* Gandy's hired all the shooters in the camp to protect the shipments his ownself—even though it hasn't done any good *yet*—and the rest of those halfways good with shootin' irons is searching these mountains for the stolen loot. Hopin' to cash it in their ownselves!" The sheriff, still holding the bottle, shook his head and dropped his shoulders. "I tell you, Hawk Haughton is fixin' to destroy this camp."

Longarm glanced up and right to see the whore staring down at him, a coquettish smile on her lips. The smile grew as she and he made eye contact. She removed the quirley from her mouth, blowing smoke and kicking her heels against the bar.

"Free drinks while you're screwin'," she said alluringly, shaking her hair back from her face.

"Candy, would you shut up?" scolded the barman. "Can't you see he ain't interested? He's a *professional*!"

"Well, I'm just so fuckin' sorry!" Candy said, dropping down from the bar, stalking to the back of the room, and haughtily climbing the stairs.

When she was gone, Longarm asked the sheriff, whose name was Hulbert Hooley, to draw him a beer.

"How 'bout a corned-beef sandwich with that?" said Hooley, indicating a big iron pot steaming on the range about fifteen feet to his right. "Only five cents extra. And while I ain't no great shakes as a lawman, I make the best corned beef this side of County Cork. It's my great-grandmother's recipe."

Longarm polished off half the beer—not bad for a mining camp hop house—before Hulbert Hooley set the corned beef on rye before him, the sandwich steaming up from a wedge of butcher paper garnished with half a pickled egg.

"The question I have for you, Sheriff," Longarm said, biting into the sandwich, then chewing a few bites before continuing, "is there any abandoned mine works around here?" He swallowed, then drank more beer. "With possibly an operational foundry?"

"Why do you ask?" said Hooley, gripping his side of the bar with both hands, one of which held a towel.

Longarm told the local badge-toter his suspicions, punctuating the telling by throwing back the rest of his beer.

"I see," said Hooley, refilling Longarm's mug at the beer keg. "By the way, how's the sandwich?"

Longarm was chewing again. He at once nodded vehemently. It was indeed one of the two or three best corned-beef-on-ryes he'd ever had.

"My great-grandmother's recipe," Hooley said again. "And to answer your question, I don't know of any abandoned mine facilities hereabouts. But I don't get out too often either. I got this saloon to run. I figure out-of-town work's what deputies are for."

"Touché," Longarm said, polishing off the sandwich.

He downed the pickled egg in a single bite. As Hooley hustled fresh beer and whiskey to the gambling miners behind Longarm, Longarm stood sideways to the bar, staring thoughtfully over the batwings toward the deep-rutted, sun-bathed street.

He sipped the beer, enjoying the dreamy feeling it gave him on top of the corned beef and the egg. About to set the heavy mug back down on the bar, he froze.

Beyond the batwings, Phil Yoakum trotted eastward along Main on a high-stepping black Thoroughbred. The man rode stiffly atop a hand-tooled saddle, coaxing the black around slower-moving supply wagons while holding the reins up close to his chest. A brace of six-guns flapped on his thighs.

Yoakum disappeared from view as Longarm shuttled his gaze to the dust-streaked window left of the batwings. Setting the beer mug on the bar, then absently tossing a silver dollar down beside it, Longarm strode swiftly through the batwings and out onto the street, staring after Yoakum.

Where could Coleridge's first lieutenant be headed, armed, in such an all-fired hurry?

The man had such a grim, furtive aspect that Longarm decided to follow him. He looked around for a saddle horse, spying one tied before the pink whorehouse across the street. For official business, he could confiscate the horse and pay its rider for his trouble, adding the cost to his expense vouchers, which Billy Vail would scowl at, of course, but what else was new?

Longarm was in the middle of the street, looking eastward, when a loud "He-yaaah!" rose behind him. A horse whinnied and a wagon clattered like thunder.

Longarm turned sharply.

The wagon he'd seen thirty seconds ago parked before the blacksmith shop barreled toward him. The dark, bearded gent in the driver's box glared at Longarm as he hoorawed the two horses in the traces, whipping the reins against their backs and yelling at the top of his lungs.

Longarm bolted toward the other side of the street. He didn't make it before the right front horse rammed its shoulder into Longarm's own, sending the lawman pinwheeling to the ground at the edge of the far boardwalk.

It wasn't much of a blow, but the horse had smacked him on the same side as the buckshot blast, and the pain sent up fiery multicolored balloons behind Longarm's eyes.

Gritting his teeth and favoring his right side, he came to his knees and looked at the wagon continuing down the street, but slowing for snarled traffic ahead.

Longarm looked around, spotted a rock, and picked it up. He flung the rock as far as he could. It sailed high, turning slowly, the sunlight catching it as it rose above the awnings of the false facades lining the street.

Longarm had little chance of hitting his target, but to his amazement, the rock fell back into the street shadows and punched through the low crown of the wagon driver's canvas hat.

The man's head snapped down as his right, gloved hand rose to his crushed hat. The wagon slowed and stopped as the driver dropped to one knee in the driver's box.

Longarm stood staring with disbelief—damn, he hadn't flung a rock in years!—then jogged ahead.

He ran around a small wagon hauling stove wood and a horseback rider regarding him curiously, and caught up to the stalled wagon. He leapt over the tailgate and into the box loaded with foodstuff, camping supplies, five brand-new rifles, and three pistol belts with shiny new .44's snugged in their holsters. Leaping a crate of forty-four shells, he scrambled over the front seat and into the driver's box.

The driver, who'd removed his hat to rub his head while pushing himself back up toward his seat, glanced warily at Longarm. "Listen, mister, I'm real sorry about that. The damn horses just plumb *bolted!*"

"That'll happen when you crack the reins over their backs and yell like the devil at Easter!" Longarm grabbed the man's collar and shuffled sideways as he threw the man over the wagon's right front wheel. With an indignant cry, the man tumbled into the street, burying his face in a pile of steaming horse apples.

Longarm leaped off the wagon, shucked his Colt from its holster, and kicked the man onto his back.

The man opened his mouth to cry, "Wait, I—"

Longarm knelt on the man's chest and held his Colt's barrel to the bridge of the man's nose. He was a short, broad-shouldered gent with straight black hair tumbling over his forehead, and belligerent, wide-spaced eyes. At the moment, the eyes were more frightened than mean.

Longarm said through gritted teeth, "You pull a stunt like that again, you're gonna regret it even more than you do now."

The man moved his lips around the barrel of Longarm's Colt. He tried to speak, but made only choking, grunting sounds.

"And you can tell your partners that going after Hawk Haughton is a poor idea. Poorer even than trying to stomp me into the street to get me out of your way. You try it, you'll be saddling a cloud and riding to the Great Beyond. Guaranteed. Understand my lingo, hombre?"

The man's oversized Adam's apple bobbed as he gagged and nodded.

Longarm removed the revolver's barrel from the man's mouth, and straightened. "Go on back to your camp and use your new toys for hunting meat, not gold."

The man climbed to his knees. He looked around at the miners and whores who'd gathered to watch the festivities. Grumbling under his breath, he wiped the horse shit from his face, then gained his feet and climbed onto his wagon.

In a minute, he was hoorawing his team eastward along Main, and the men and ladies, still snickering, sauntered back to their shops, saloons, and whorehouses.

All but one whore, that is. The redhead who'd been showing off her ass to the three miners sidled up to Longarm and draped her wrist over his shoulder, leaning against him seductively, snugging her breasts against his shoulder.

"I got a secret, Deputy Long."

Longarm looked down at her. Her blue eyes were pretty beneath the false eyelashes. The beauty mark of a diamond-shaped mole adorned her right cheekbone. She smiled and sucked the half-dissolved rock candy on her tongue, the mint fragrance wafting across his face.

"Don't we all?"

"I got one that's gonna interest you in partic'lar." The redhead glanced around cautiously, then, still smiling, said quietly, "It's about Hawk Haughton, that bastard son of a bitch!"

Chapter 14

Longarm arched an eyebrow at the redheaded whore star-ing up at him. As he opened his mouth to speak, she pressed two fingers to his lips.

"Not out here." She smiled woodenly, keeping her voice low as she grabbed his arm like it was a pole she were about to climb. "Wouldn't want it to get around I fuck and tell. What do you say you and me mosey inside and get comfortable?"

Longarm let the redhead lead him through the front door of the pink whorehouse. They moved through a small saloon area in which two men in watch caps were playing checkers, down a short hall, and into a room with several mismatched fainting couches, a sofa, and piano.

It was a shabby place, with thin rugs on the floor and the sour fetor of alcohol, smoke, and sex. Longarm had never much cared for brothels of any kind, but from what he'd seen so far, this was one of the better houses of ill repute in Lulu City.

Apparently, the madame agreed—judging by the rates painted on a plain wooden board hung on the pine-paneled wall between two windows.

Men's voices sounded upstairs, above the forlorn song a

girl was singing slightly out of tune. Out back, a dog was barking. In the room Longarm shared with the redhead, a black-and-white cat sat atop a scarred piano bench and licked its paw, then used the paw to clean behind its right ear.

As Longarm sank into the sofa, holding his hat in his hands, the whore sat down beside him, curling one bare leg beneath her hip.

"Miss, if you wanna share secrets—"

The girl cut him off again by throwing herself into his arms and mashing her mouth down on his.

In the hall outside the parlor, men's heavily accented voices boomed, and thick-soled boots pounded the floor. Looking around the whore in his arms as she pasted her lips to his, Longarm glanced at the doorway.

Two men and a skinny Indian girl in a bright red dress wandered past, one of the men with his right arm draped around the girl's shoulders.

When boots resounded on creaky stairs, the redhead drew away from Longarm and pulled her corset up higher on her breasts. "It's your lucky day," she said, using her index finger to wipe spittle from the right corner of his mouth. "Normally, I charge a nickel a kiss."

"As I was sayin'," Longarm said, "if you wanna share secrets, wouldn't a private room make better sense?"

"If we were to go upstairs, someone might think I hauled you up there for privacy. I don't intend to get private. Too many people got their eye on you, and those who know I did business with Haughton might think I ratted him out."

When more voices sounded in the hall, the redhead slid closer to Longarm and pushed her hand against his crotch. She snugged her cheek against his, whispering, "I fucked Haughton a few weeks back, when the gang was hangin' around town like they owned the place. He let slip while pie-eyed that him and his gang were holed up in a canyon, and the only way into the canyon from this side is through a long tunnel in a mountain."

Longarm winced as she massaged his dong through his trousers. "He was braggin' how no one could ever track him there. And even if they did, a whole army couldn't root him out."

Longarm removed the girl's hand so he could think straight. "He say where this tunnel was exactly?"

The whore shook her head, brown eyes regarding him expectantly. "That's all he said. I was hoping it might help. If he keeps preyin' on the Holy Smokes gold, Lulu City ain't long for this world. And I like it here. I'm makin' the most money I ever made."

"He didn't even say *which* direction this tunnel is from town?"

"I didn't wanna prod him, make him suspicious. He pays well for a poke, though he's the most disgusting creature I've ever spread my legs for."

The whore shuddered and wrinkled her nose. "He smells like he bathes in pig shit. Someone might know about the tunnel he mentioned even though I don't. Maybe some of the old salts still breakin' rock in the mountains . . ."

Longarm donned his hat. He didn't have much time before the gold shipped tomorrow, but it was something to go on anyway. And like she said, someone in town might know of such a tunnel.

Longarm sighed and slapped the girl's bare thigh. "I'm much obliged for the help, uh . . ."

"Lil."

Longarm looked at her curiously.

The redhead grinned, showing a gap where an eyetooth had been. "Lulu City Lil. Nicest ass west of Colorado Springs!"

He leaned over and kissed her cheek. "It is indeed, Lil."

As Longarm stood, her eyes followed his crotch. "Reckon I got you worked up. Want me to suck you off?"

"No, thanks." Longarm headed for the door. "I'll just wash my face in the creek."

•　　•　　•

Longarm spent the rest of the afternoon milling about town, patronizing the saloons and gambling parlors, gently pumping miners, barkeeps, and whores for information about long tunnels through mountain walls and any other clues the Haughton Gang might have sprinkled around Lulu City while frequenting the town's brothels and hop houses.

It turned out to be a waste of time. The old prospectors merely shook their heads dully when he inquired about tunnels and remote canyons. So did Sheriff Hooley, again making the excuse that he didn't get out much and that's what deputies were for.

Around seven o'clock, when the shadows had once more spilled down from the ridges and he'd sent a telegram to Billy Vail in Denver, updating his boss on the current situation in Lulu City, Longarm headed back to the London Hotel.

Ma McBryde cooked him a big steak with all the trimmings. Later that night, when he was sound asleep, there was a tap on his door. He answered it naked, because that's how he always slept, grabbing his .44 but not cocking it.

Perfume wafted under the door. He set the gun down and let Zeena in, her breasts jutting between the flaps of her open wrapper as she threw herself into his arms.

"Oh, Custis, why can't I get enough of you?"

Longarm chuckled and tossed her onto the bed.

They had a fine old time, but he kicked her out after an hour, telling her he needed his beauty sleep. He woke at five-thirty the next morning, his inner alarm as dependable as any Big Ben, then dressed and headed out into the cool, predawn darkness.

He found a tiny, earthen-floored eatery on a side street, owned and run by a taciturn Chinaman. After a hefty serving of sidepork, sausage, scrambled eggs, and dumplings filled with spiced meat—all of it washed down with bitter coffee and punctuated by a half-smoked cigar—he tipped the Chinaman and sauntered over to the livery barn.

He got the livery owner out of the mattress sack to saddle a stout, deep-bottomed grulla gelding. Minutes later, he followed the narrow-gauge track out of town as the sky over the eastern ridges turned lilac, dimming the stars.

He'd had Hulbert Hooley and one of Hooley's regular customers, a seasoned prospector named Murray Lester, draw him a map of the passable ridges along the narrow-gauge track meandering down the mountains toward Colorado Springs. Longarm intended to follow the line as closely as he could, keeping to the ridges and mountainsides above, where he'd be more likely to spot trouble and also more likely to warn the train's engineer with wood smoke, and send him chugging back to Lulu City.

If Longarm spotted anything out of the ordinary out here—anything except black squirrels, white jays, and bear shit—he'd signal the train and start tracking.

He'd crossed two saddles and a deep valley along ice-rimed Lulu Creek when he heard the distant chugs of the train. He kept following the track for another couple of miles, looking around for shod hoofprints, fresh spoor, or cigarette butts—any sign of the train robbers—then turned the horse down to the creek for water.

Sun winked off the ice and snow lining the creek. Longarm squinted up the canyon wall as the train chugged into view—only an engine, a wood tender, express car, and caboose. Pushing along at maybe fifteen miles an hour, it followed the rail bed blasted out of the side of the ridge, about fifty feet up from the creek. As the grulla slurped water and twitched its ears at the train's roar, the wheels clacking and screeching on the iron rails, Longarm threw out an arm. The engineer stuck his head out of the locomotive's window and returned the wave.

There was a water stop a couple of miles away, on the other side of a steep grade. Longarm would catch up with the train there, then continue scouting ahead. A man traveling horseback as the crow flies could stay ahead of a train in this up-and-down country.

It was starting to look as though Haughton wasn't going to show anyway. Longarm would probably be up here till next fall, hunting those privy rats. . . .

He watched the train follow the curving ridge into the next segment of canyon and slip from view, its diamond stack spewing acrid black vapor. He dropped to a knee, removed his hat, and splashed water over his face. A few minutes later, he was mounted up and riding again along the canyon's rocky floor.

The ground suddenly shook beneath the grulla's hooves.

A blast resounded, like the sound of several lightning bolts striking a tree. The booming report chased its own echoes around the ridges.

Longarm drew back on the grulla's reins and stared into the mouth of the narrow canyon ahead and left, obscured by a bend in the creek bed. He couldn't see much. Beyond the protruding mountain wall, men were shouting, rifles popping.

Above the din rose a tooth-gnashing screech, like that of big steel canisters being squeezed by a giant's fist.

Longarm grimaced. *"Shit!"*

He booted the horse into a trot, its hooves clomping and slipping along the rocks. As more gunshots resounded, as though a small battle were raging in the bottle neck of the canyon a half mile ahead, Longarm turned the grulla up a game trail etching the mountain wall and meandering through talus slides, brush, and scrub pines.

Best to approach the train robbers from the ridge shoulder, where he'd have a better vantage, than from the canyon floor.

He kept the horse moving at a good clip, snapping curses under his breath, but resisted the urge to whip the horse with his rein ends. There was no point in risking breaking one of the grulla's legs, and being set afoot out here.

No doubt because of the trouble the woodcutters and

Longarm had given the gang earlier, Hawk Haughton must have gotten extra cautious. He'd probably expected tighter security around the shipment. That's why'd he struck so far from Lulu City.

If Longarm only had a few extra, trained guns on his side . . .

He continued into a thick stand of barren aspen growing along a frozen spring on the mountain's shoulder. The smell of steam and cordite wafted through the trees, and men's yells rose.

Longarm dismounted, shucked his Winchester, and ran forward, dropped to a knee behind a lightning-struck cedar, and peered into the boulder-choked canyon below.

The train lay amongst the boulders in a heap of shattered wood and twisted steel, obscured by steam and dust and the smoke from the dynamite the gang had obviously used to blow the tracks. Broken rails hung down the slope, as if to point out the train wreckage below.

Men and horses moved inside the steam. Angry shouts and shrill whinnies sounded. Occasional rocks, dislodged by the blast, rolled down the slope and into the canyon, booming against the wreckage.

Someone was screaming as though in excruciating pain.

The gunfire had died except for occasional pistol pops. On the heels of a shot, the screaming died abruptly.

Snugging the Winchester's butt against his cheek, Longarm tried to get a bead on a moving figure. No use. The smoke, dust, and steam were still too thick to make out features.

He'd have to get closer.

He was outnumbered by a dozen to one, but he wasn't about to sit here and watch those murdering bastards ride off with the gold. . . .

He stepped out from the tree and, crouching, holding the Winchester high across his chest, dropped over the cut bank. It was a ten-foot drop.

He landed flat-footed, knees bent, behind a boulder. Moving quickly out from behind the rock and using the thick webs of dust and steam for cover, he approached the demolished train. The outlaws' voices grew louder but the words were just as indiscernible, as several were talking at once.

Suddenly, silence. Only the sound of hissing steam, clomping horses, and squeaking tack.

"Told ye they were gonna try somethin' like this sooner or later!" a man shouted, his voice cracking.

"Fuck you, Ephraim!"

"Fuck you, brother! Let's get the hell outta here!"

As hooves thumped and more tack squawked, as if men were mounting, Longarm jogged up to the corrugated tin roof of the overturned express car.

He ducked down, peering over the lip of the roof. Beyond, a dozen or so riders were trotting and cantering off through the sifting dust, their horses clattering on the rocks and patches of dirty snow and ice. They were a ragged, heavily armed bunch on fine, heavy-rumped horses bred for fast mountain travel.

Longarm extended the Winchester, drawing a bead on the back of a buffalo coat. Inside the express car, someone groaned.

Longarm held the shot, raised the Winchester's barrel, and leaped onto the side of the car. He hunkered down beside the heavy steel door that had been twisted half off in the wreck, and peered through the gap.

Three men lay in bloody heaps at the far end of the car. One lifted his chin to glare up at Longarm, gray eyes reflecting the midday light. He spat a curse and winced before his lids closed over his eyes, and his chin dipped down to his bloody chest.

Longarm cast his glance about the car. Except for the three guards, a few folding chairs, lunch boxes, and a broken milk bottle, the car was bare.

Squinting against the dust and smoke, Longarm looked

around the rocks and strewn rubble around the train. Several more bullet-riddled bodies lay about the canyon. Judging by the size of several wounds, some of the guards had been shot at close range, probably after they were already incapacitated. Scuff marks told that at least one had been dragged out of the express car before he was shot in the back of the head.

As he leaped off the express car and strode around the wreckage, finding the bodies of the engineer and fireman—one of which was crushed by the locomotive—Longarm spotted the two lockboxes about twenty feet down canyon from the hot, steaming engine and the wood tender still spewing thick clouds of acrid blue smoke.

The locks on both boxes had been shot off, the lids opened. As Longarm stared down into one and then the other, hot bile churned in his gut.

The boxes weren't empty. The gang had had little use for what they'd found inside:

Thirty worthless bars of lead.

Chapter 15

Longarm scrambled around the rocks and wreckage at the bottom of the canyon, eventually discovering four bodies in addition to Gandy's six guards.

All were dead. They'd either been killed when the train had been blown off the track and rolled down the canyon wall, or shot by Hawk Haughton's bunch.

Deciding it was too late to start tracking the gang—it would be good dark in three hours—Longarm gathered the dead and mounded rocks over them to keep predators away, then retrieved his horse and turned him back up the canyon toward Lulu City.

It was a three-hour ride back the way he'd come, and he passed the time imagining ways of killing Gandy and Coleridge slowly, savoring every second. Not telling him about the dummy run of lead in place of the gold, they'd played him for a fool. Had they told the men who'd died in the wreck? Probably not. Who'd knowingly hang their asses over the fire for 150 pounds of lead?

Longarm laughed dryly as he stopped to let the grulla draw water from the creek. Then he sobered. If the train had been carrying only lead, where in the hell was the gold?

He drank from the stream, the water so cold it gave him a headache, then mounted up and rode the last few miles to Lulu City in near-darkness. He rode through town, only vaguely hearing the banjos and mouth organs playing in the saloons, the squeals of the women, the laughter of the drunken miners.

In the mountains north of town, coyotes yammered, and several dogs howled back.

He didn't like being played for a fool. Especially not by those he'd come to help.

Longarm stopped in town only long enough to inform the sheriff of the train debacle down canyon, and that he'd better get a crew down there for the bodies first thing in the morning.

Entertaining no questions, Longarm swung into the leather again and trotted the grulla into the buttes north of Lulu City. He followed a wide bend through cedar-tufted scarps. Ahead, the Gandy cabin's front windows shone with lamplight, and smoke spewed from the stout rock chimney, tingeing the chill pine-perfumed air with the smell of burning cedar and seasoned beef.

Longarm drew the grulla up to the hitching post, before which a glistening black surrey sat beside a saddled, blaze-faced dun. Longarm glanced at the leather-seated rig, and gave a snort. Coleridge was here. Good. The more, the merrier.

He took the three porch steps in a single bound and threw open the door without knocking.

"Longarm!" exclaimed Rose Gandy, dropping the cup of coffee she was about to hand her betrothed, sitting a chair near the big stone hearth.

To Coleridge's left sat his assistant, the mysterious Phil Yoakum, who had a Hopkins and Allen pocket pistol in his right fist, aimed at Longarm. The man's scowling face was beet-red.

Yoakum's pearl-gripped .32 sagged as Gandy, kneeling before the fire with a split log in one hand and an iron poker in the other, turned his head toward the open door. "What the . . . ?"

Longarm stepped into the cabin and kicked the door closed. He didn't bother wiping his feet on the braided hemp rug just beyond the threshold. "Surprised to see me?" He glanced at Yoakum, who'd lowered the popgun but whose eyes remained hard and cunning. "You're right fast with that little popgun, Phil. Very fast for a mine works secretary."

Tossing the log into the fire, Solomon Gandy straightened to his full six and a half feet, and stared at Longarm. "What happened?"

"What do you think?" Longarm pulled a cigar from his shirt pocket, walked over to the lamp beside Yoakum, and touched it to the hot cylinder.

Puffing smoke, he turned to Gandy. "They blew the train off the tracks, killed everybody. A few might have lived, but the renegades were so piss-burned when they found your lead staring up at 'em from those lockboxes, they went ahead and shot 'em all."

Rose gasped and looked up from her crouch over the coffee spill and the broken cup and saucer.

"You act as though this is my fault," Gandy scoffed.

"I don't like being played for a mooncalf. Did those men on the train know they were hauling lead?"

Gandy just stared at him. Coleridge and Yoakum glanced at each other, their expressions inscrutable.

Yoakum slipped the Hopkins and Allen into an unseen shoulder holster beneath his frock. "They were adequately paid."

"Most men like to know what they're dying for. I sure as hell like to know what I'm risking my life for. Jerking the strings of a federal lawman might not be technically against the law, but it's sure a good way to piss-burn me. And when I'm piss-burned, I tend to forget I'm a lawman."

"Are you threatening me, Deputy Long?" asked Gandy, nostrils flaring.

"Yes."

For the first time, Ebeneezer Coleridge spoke, after clearing his throat against his fist. "Those men we hired to guard the train were . . . not exactly model citizens, Deputy Long. Most of them were or had been outlaws themselves."

"The earth's a better place without 'em," Gandy added, setting the poker into a rack beside the hearth.

Longarm glared at him, puffing smoke. "What Bible verse is that from?"

"This isn't getting us anywhere, gentlemen," Yoakum said, standing and turning to Longarm. "The point is, the gold is being safely transported to Colorado Springs."

"How?"

"Mule train," said Coleridge, remaining seated. "The other guards we hired are taking it down an old prospectors' trail. It's longer and slower, but it isn't likely Hawk Haughton will ever find them now that they've gotten a good head start."

Longarm stared at the towheaded youngster, rolling the cigar in his lips, thinking it over. Finally, he sighed and looked at Yoakum. "I reckon if it doesn't make it safe and sound to Colorado Springs, you've got a spy on your hands, Mr. Gandy."

Yoakum narrowed his eyes. "What's that supposed to mean, Long?"

"It means I don't like the way you smell, Phil. I've seen your face before, just can't remember where. Something tells me it's on a wanted circular. But I reckon that's neither here nor there . . . for now." Longarm turned and headed for the door.

"What're you going to do, Longarm?" Rose called.

At the door, Longarm turned back. Rose stood beside Coleridge, the broken cup in her hand. She stared at Longarm, surprise and expectation in her face as she thrust her shoulders back, pushing her small breasts out.

Coleridge glanced up at her, frown lines creasing his forehead. Gandy turned to her too, obviously miffed.

131

"I'm gonna take a long, hot bath, then eat a steak, Miss Rose." He glanced at Gandy. "The sheriff's gonna retrieve the bodies from the train wreck first thing in the morning. I told him you'd supply him with men and wagons."

With that, he turned through the open door, went out, mounted up, and headed back toward Lulu City.

The town's lights were just rising above the slope's shoulder, and Longarm had just bent forward to relight his cheroot, when a bullet screeched off a boulder on the right side of the trail.

In the dense mountain silence, the rifle report echoed like a howitzer blast.

The echo hadn't died before Longarm kicked his boots free of the stirrups and threw himself to the ground. As the horse buck-kicked, whinnied, and bolted down the trail, its flailing rear hooves missing Longarm by a hairbreadth, the lawman rolled behind the same boulder the bullet had drilled.

His cocked .44 in his right hand, he peered around the boulder's left side. Venom burned as he tried to pierce the darkness with his gaze.

"Yoakum!" he raked out. "Come on out and show yourself, you bushwhacking son of a bitch!"

As if in reply, another bullet plowed into the boulder before Longarm, spraying shards, the rifle report echoing and setting dogs to barking amongst the old prospectors' shacks studding the hills. Longarm had seen the gun flash about thirty yards up a low hill on the other side of the trail.

He extended his pistol around the boulder, and fired. A second later, another flash, and Longarm drew his head back behind the boulder, squinting as more shards flew around him.

He looked around. To his right, several junipers and cedars dropped away to a low wash.

He raised the revolver once more, snapped off two quick shots, then scrambled along behind the shrubs and dropped into the wash. It was only a foot-deep trough twisting along the slope's shoulder. He crabbed eastward, keeping his head low, sliding the Winchester along in his right hand, so starlight winking off the barrel wouldn't give him away.

He'd moved about fifty yards before scrambling up out of the wash, crouching behind a dwarf cedar, and filling his Colt's empty cylinders from his cartridge belt. He held his breath, watching and listening.

Seeing no movement around the hill, and hearing no footsteps, he spun the cylinder and sprinted straight ahead, then leaped over the shoulder's crest to the other side.

Before him, starlight winked off metal. Crouching, he fired three quick shots. All three shots sparked and clanged.

Longarm froze, powder smoke wafting around his head.

Galloping hooves thudded into the distance as dogs and coyotes yipped and howled. Longarm stepped forward, saw that what he'd shot at was a discarded, rusty wheel rim half-buried at the base of the hill.

As the hoof thuds died, Longarm climbed the hill. Near the crest, he crouched down, picked up the three spent cartridges, jingled them in his hand as he stared westward. He saw nothing but black clumps of shrubs and rocks in the velvet darkness lidded with a billion stars.

The rider was heading toward Gandy's mine works.

It had to be Yoakum. Who else knew he'd be out here? Yoakum had wanted to shoot Longarm earlier; the lawman had seen it in the man's eyes. Longarm could go back up to Gandy's shack, try pumping the others for answers. But they probably didn't know anything more about Yoakum than Longarm did.

Had Coleridge's assistant thrown in with Hawk and Ephraim Haughton? Longarm remembered seeing the man cantering businesslike down Main Street yesterday, with two pistols on his hips. If he had thrown his iron into the Haughtons' fire, he'd probably been heading out to alert them about the gold shipment.

Wait a minute.

There hadn't been a gold shipment. Haughton had hit the decoy train. . . .

Surely Yoakum had known of Gandy's and Coleridge's plans. . . .

Longarm made a sour expression and spat, as if to rid the taste of confusion from his tongue. His head was spinning, and it wasn't from hitting the ground so hard either.

He should go back to Gandy's cabin and sound Gandy and Coleridge out about Yoakum, but nothing would come together until Longarm had found out where the gang was stashing the gold.

Longarm holstered his pistol, hitched his gun belt higher on his hips, smoothed his sheepskin down over the grips, and walked over the crest of the hill. His ass was dragging from frustration and fatigue. He'd been duped and used by Gandy.

But then again, if gold had been on that train, Haughton would have nabbed it. With Longarm alone, there wouldn't have been much he could have done to stop him.

Longarm sighed deeply. This was as tough a knot as he'd ever faced. But Billy wouldn't have sent him if the marshal hadn't thought Longarm could handle it.

Breath puffing in the chill air, he picked up the trail, followed it to where his horse was standing, still looking skittish, in an aspen clump, and mounted up.

A half hour later, Longarm stepped into the antechamber of the London Hotel. The old desk clerk, Sandy, was digging grit from under his fingernails with a folding barlow knife. He looked up as Longarm shut the door behind him.

"Well, look what the bobcat dragged back to the cave. She must have a large litter to pull back a carcass big as you!" Pleased with himself, Sandy laughed, shoulders shaking beneath his shabby serge coat, one eye nearly hidden by a lock of brown hair.

Longarm heard hushed women's voices in another room. Zeena and another woman were having after-supper coffee, chatting politely. Cups clicked against saucers. The aromas of roast beef and gravy tinged the fresher smell of the coffee.

Longarm tossed Sandy a ten-dollar gold piece as he headed for the stairs. "Will that cover a steak and a bath in my room?"

"Ain't got much choice. I doubt Ma would want you sittin' in one of her nice dining room chairs, filthy as you are." Sandy pocketed the coin. Longarm was on the stairs. "What do you want first?"

"The bath."

"You got it."

A half hour later, Longarm was sitting in the copper tub, soaping himself, when the door clicked. He glanced behind him, expecting to see Sandy with another bucket. It was Zeena. She wore a black kimono-style shift.

"Slow night, so I let Sandy go early," Zeena said as she closed the door, then poured the water into the tub between's Longarm's legs, the robe opening to expose the deep, creamy cleavage. "I'll bring your steak up when you give the word. Look at your back! What have you been up to, Custis?"

"No damn good at all!" he groused, punching the water, the soapy liquid spraying his face and burning his right eye. He cursed again.

"Those wounds are going to need new wraps. I'll do it later, when there's no chance of opening them up again."

She smiled, removed the robe, and stepped into the tub. Her nipples jutted from her big, full globes as she sank down opposite Longarm, drawing her knees to her chest. She'd already pinned her hair into a loose bun atop her head.

Suddenly, Longarm's eye didn't burn so much. She must have seen the confounded expression in his face, however. She frowned. "Wanna tell me about it?"

"No."

He grabbed her ankles, pulled her legs up and over his

thighs. She gave a surprised gasp. Suddenly, her breasts were pressed against his chest and his shaft was probing her nether regions. He kissed her, drew away. "Maybe later."

"Whatever you want," she breathed, her eyes rolling as she ran her hands through his hair, his rock-hard shaft sliding home.

Chapter 16

Early the next morning, as the false dawn lifted a milky wash behind the eastern peaks, Longarm placed his hand on the shoulder of the Occidental Livery Barn's snoring proprietor.

"Rise and shine, old-timer," Longarm said, giving the man's right shoulder a jerk.

Burk Dane snapped his head up from his cot. In the soft, flickering light from Longarm's lantern, the man blinked with surprise. "Jesus Christ, what is it? Who's there?" He reached for his glasses and slipped his right foot off the cot. "The barn on fire? I don't smell smoke!"

"The barn ain't on fire. I need another horse. A real stayer this time."

Folding his glasses back behind his ears, Dane blinked up at Longarm. He wore threadbare balbriggans and thick, wool socks pulled up to his knees. His wavy, pewter gray hair was sticking up like bristles on a tumbleweed.

"Christ, can't you keep regular hours?"

"These are regular hours."

"Our lawman, Hulbert Hooley, he ain't much for law enforcin', but at least the man don't wake a body up just after he's gone to bed!"

The old man heaved himself up from the cot, stepped into his overalls while cursing under his breath, then staggered sleepily into the main part of the barn.

He saddled a svelte buckskin, then stood back as Longarm fashioned packs from the two sacks of trail supplies and food that Zeena had provided, and tied one to the cantle, the other to the pommel. The lawman lashed his rifle scabbard over the right stirrup, the Winchester's butt facing forward and up, within easy reach.

Longarm paid Burk Dane two days' rent in advance along with a half-eagle tip—all on Uncle Sam, of course—and Dane shook his head, incredulous, as the lawman led the horse into the quiet street, mounted up, and trotted briskly eastward through smoke wisping from fledgling breakfast fires.

"You mind that buckskin," Dane called. "He's the best in my remuda!"

Longarm made good time retracing yesterday's route to the canyon into which the train had been blasted from the rails. The sun was full up and splashing crisp copper light onto the twisted, broken wreckage as Longarm rode down to pick up Hawk Haughton's tracks. The bodies had started to smell in spite of the cold night beneath the rocks, and of course the birds had found the rock pile.

Screeching magpies probed the gaps between the rocks as Longarm walked the buckskin past, leaning out to follow the shod hoofprints of Haughton's dozen-plus riders. The tracks followed the canyon for nearly two miles, then climbed northward up a steep trough in the ridge, and down the other side of the mountain, through tall pines, oaks, spruce, and tamaracks.

In a deep valley on the other side, cut by a fast-moving stream that would likely be a raging millrace when the snow on the higher peaks started melting, the tracks faded abruptly, as though they'd been expertly brushed out.

Longarm reined the buckskin to a halt, stared pensively at the stream rushing between sharply cut banks lined with dead willows and red-brown ferns, only deer and coyote prints marking the half-frozen mud at the edge of the water. The bastards were sneaky, accustomed to being trailed—old veterans of the long coulees and Appalachian hollows.

Longarm had been down those coulees a few times himself.

He clucked to the horse and continued downstream. Where the banks narrowed, he found some pocked turf and freshly broken deadfall, several limbs hanging from aspens by bark strands. Men had ridden through here.

Longarm jumped the buckskin across. Fifteen minutes later, he again found Haughton's horse tracks, and followed the sign across a gently sloping meadow carpeted in spindly, winter-dormant aspens in which chickadees and nuthatches piped.

The lawman threaded a course between dirty snowdrifts peppered with elk or deer pellets, his eyes picking up the deep indentations left by iron shoes and the fresh horse apples spotting the drifts and the frozen rivulets between.

A half hour later, however, the gang had covered their trail again. Longarm zigzagged over several hogbacks, cursing and staring at the ground as though looking for bread crumbs in bramble patches.

"Foxy sons of bitches."

Hoof thuds sounded. Longarm stared into the gently sloping canyon below and left. Through towering pines, two figures moved. They came on rapidly, a girl laughing, a young man calling to her.

Longarm backed the buckskin behind a thumb of gray, moss-spotted rock poking up from the hogback.

The girl laughed again. "Come on—it's this way, Mr. Coleridge, sir!"

"Rose, dang blast it, how far are you going to lead me? We're gonna get lost."

"I know this country like the back of my hand," Rose called to her beau, Ebeneezer Coleridge, galloping behind

139

her. "You forget—I grew up out here. Come on!" Directly behind Longarm and crouched low in her saddle, skirts whipping about her stirrups, Rose laughed and continued on past, her horse—the same one Gandy had ridden the other day—snorting and shaking its head.

Longarm hung back until Coleridge, clad in a blue wool coat over his customary serge suit, complete with bowler, round spectacles, and black half-boots, had galloped on down the trail, the soft thuds of his horse's hooves echoing faintly behind him.

Longarm stared after the two, perplexed. What in the hell were they doing this far from Lulu City? This was dangerous country to be out frolicking like forest sprites. They probably just wanted to get out from under the thumb of pious, old Gandy for a day, but what was Coleridge doing with a day off so soon after the gold shipment?

Deciding to find out, Longarm booted the buckskin down the hogback and onto the game trail scarred by Rose and Ebeneezer's galloping horses. He rode for a hundred yards, then halted the buckskin.

Rose and Coleridge's horses stood along the trail, ground-tied. They swished their tails and turned their heads toward Longarm, who dismounted, dropped the buckskin's reins, and strode into the woods left of the trail, following the sound of giggling.

Longarm stepped down a natural levee, walked quietly into the trees. He didn't want to be spied just yet, before he knew what the two younkers were up to out here, so close to Hawk Haughton's trail.

Longarm followed the sound of hushed voices and muffled laughter. Suddenly, he swerved behind a broad balsam fir, then shuttled a glance around the left side of the tree, holding a bough down with his left hand.

Twenty yards beyond, Ebeneezer Coleridge stood facing Longarm. The younker's hat was off, his pants and silk underwear down around his ankles.

Rose knelt before him, hands raised to his crotch. Her

140

head moved up and down, a prim little straw hat pinned to her hair. Ebeneezer tipped his own head back on his shoulders, and groaned with pleasure.

Longarm released the balsam bough, his lips shaping a sheepish smile. He'd give them a few minutes, then move in and find out why the young'uns couldn't be practicing their French a little closer to home.

He turned to head back to his horse. He hadn't turned full around before a brass-butted rifle stock was thrust toward him. It rammed into his head, instantly setting about six banjos to playing out of tune in his brain, and turning the forest around him upside down.

Longarm dropped to his knees. His head wobbled on his shoulders as he lifted his gaze. A man stood before him— black-clad and wearing an eye patch.

Phil Yoakum grinned down at him, and clucked. "A man your age spying on children. You oughta be ashamed."

Longarm swiped his hand toward his .44. Again, Yoakum swung the rifle around, the butt tattooing Longarm's right temple. Longarm hit the ground on his shoulder, the world coming in and out of focus as a veil of red closed over his eyes.

Everything went black for a time, and then he found himself on his back, staring up.

Rose crouched over him. Behind him, Ebeneezer Coleridge was tucking his shirt into his pants, looking bemused and devilish.

"We saw you coming a ways back," she said, her words sounding far away as her face came in and out of focus. "They wanted to shoot you out of your saddle. I told them we could do this without killing you, but first we had to lure you in." She stared down at him, her hazel eyes vaguely regretful. "What I'm trying to say is, you have me to thank you're still alive."

Longarm gritted his teeth. "What's the game? You three . . . in with Haughton?"

Yoakum laced his fingers around her arm and slid his rifle barrel toward Longarm's face. Longarm's revolver was wedged behind Yoakum's cartridge belt. He wondered vaguely if he still had his derringer in his coat pocket.

"Step away, Rose," ordered Yoakum. He glanced at Coleridge. "Should we go ahead and kill him?"

"No!" Rose said, standing and turning to the one-eyed man, her fists balled at her sides. "I told you, I don't want him killed. He was good to me on the train, and I will not let you kill him. There's been enough killing."

"Just how good *was* he on the train, Rose?" asked Ebeneezer Coleridge, frowning behind his glasses. "Not so good he let you give him one of your French lessons, I hope!"

Rose had turned her angry gaze to her future husband. "Ebeneezer, are you calling me a whore?"

"I just wanna know what I'm marryin', that's all."

"Save it for the honeymoon, kids," Yoakum said. Holding his rifle on Longarm, he turned to Rose. "Killing a lawman'll probably bring others, but I don't see another way."

"There's another digging near the one where your men stashed the gold. A deeper one." Rose stared beseechingly at Yoakum. "We'll bind him and throw him in there. By the time he can free himself, we'll be long gone."

Yoakum lowered his Winchester. Scowling at Rose, he thrust the rifle at Coleridge. "Hold this on him while I fetch the horses."

When Yoakum had left, Longarm squinted up at the two youngsters staring down at him, Coleridge squinting over the rifle's barrel. The gun made the kid nervous. Sweat streaked his smooth-shaven, peaches-and-cream cheeks. "This sure is gonna be a disappointment to your old man, Rose," said Longarm.

"Fuck the old bastard," snapped Coleridge.

Longarm cast his incredulous gaze at Rose. "Why?"

Rose reached down and flecked dirt and dead grass from the side of Longarm's head, gently, but her eyes were hard, her jaws set. "Papa will probably live to be a hundred . . . thumping that damn Bible every minute. He wants me to come back to Lulu City and teach school and keep house for him."

"He treats us both like slaves." Coleridge breathed sharply as he kept the rifle stock snugged to his cheek.

"He's kept me on a short leash because of his money," Rose continued. "Now his money is mine, and Ebeneezer and I are getting out of Colorado."

"Sounds like a penny-dreadful yarn, Miss Rose."

"Actually, more like something Mr. Dumas would write. Full of exotic adventures. Of course, those are still to come. . . ."

Longarm tried to lift his head. It felt like two hundred pounds of solid steel, and the blow had made him sick to his stomach. He resigned himself to inertia, staring up at Coleridge. "Don't think I'd trust ole Hawk Haughton, though. Wouldn't put it past him to light out with your share."

"You're wrong about that, lawman," said Yoakum, riding in on his tall black and leading Rose and Ebeneezer's mounts by their bridle reins. "Whatever else he might be, Hawk's honest. *Our* family's always been honest, in spite of our choosing opposing sides during the Little Misunderstanding."

He dismounted, grabbed his lariat from his saddle horn, and cut a two-foot length with a pocketknife.

Longarm's head pounded worse than before. "*Our* family?"

"Me, Hawk, and Ephraim"—Yoakum grinned at Longarm as he cut a second two-foot length from the lariat—"we're first cousins. Went our separate ways durin' the war, but we see eye-to-eye now, pardon the quip. Hawk, Ephraim, and I are organizing our own army in Mexico. In about ten years, you'll be working for a new government."

"Shit," Longarm chuckled mirthlessly. "You're Phil *Haughton*!"

"Yoakum was my mama's maiden name."

"Why in the hell couldn't I place you? Aide-de-camp to Sherman, my ass. You were a Union turncoat, took to killing farmers in Kansas and Nebraska, and robbed banks and trains after the war. Lost your eye to a bank guard's shotgun."

"That was before me and my cousins joined forces . . . decided to take over the country!" Yoakum laughed crazily.

"You boys have been mixing too much strychnine in your corn squeezings," Longarm grunted, his mind spinning from the braining and the absurdity of the Haughton boys' endeavor.

"Shut up!" Yoakum crouched beside him, smacked his head with the back of his hand. While Coleridge held the rifle barrel six inches from Longarm's head, the would-be revolutionary brusquely turned the lawman onto his belly and tied his hands behind his back.

"We will carry out our plans," Yoakum insisted, breathing hard, excited with the prospect. "We got the men and the money. With the money we'll buy the guns and more men down in Mexico!"

"What about the stamp?" Longarm asked. "You can't sell the gold with Gandy's stamp."

Coleridge laughed.

"Shut up," Rose ordered.

"I reckon if we tell you any more, Longarm," said Coleridge as Yoakum tied the lawman's ankles together, "we'll have to kill you. Can't help bein' proud, though. We thought this thing out rather well."

Longarm looked up at Rose, his jaws tight with anger. "You realize you're assisting lunatic revolutionaries?"

"If it weren't for them," Rose said, "Ebeneezer and I would be slaves of my father till we'd each gone to our deathbeds. He's evil. I bare the scars from his whip and his quirt to prove it. Besides, I don't worry my head about what goes on south of the border."

Yoakum chuckled as he jerked Longarm to his feet. "And right you shouldn't, Miss Rose. Once my cousin and

I have established our own new government, you and Ebe-neezer will be rasing a whole passel of young'uns in South America."

"Shut up, Phil!" exclaimed Coleridge, lowering the rifle and glaring at Yoakum.

The one-eyed man sucked air through his teeth, feigning chagrin. "Whoops! Damn. Me and my big mouth." He laughed as he crouched, wrapped his arms around Long-arm's knees, and heaved him up over the saddle of Co-leridge's horse. "Oh, well, I didn't say *which* country in South America. It's a big continent, you know."

Lying belly-down across the saddle, Longarm bit down hard on his back molars as Coleridge led the horse afoot up the slope through the towering pines. Yoakum rode point while Rose kept her horse back with Longarm, reining around the close-growing trees. A large carpetbag hung down from her saddle horn.

Pain shot from the top of the lawman's head, down his neck and back, through his legs, and into his toes. Shame lanced him like a dull knife. He should have known he'd been led into a trap, just as he should have remembered he'd seen Yoakum's face on a half-dozen wanted circulars over the past ten years.

Longarm lifted his pounding head, regarding Gandy's daughter through slitted eyes. They'd mentioned gold stashed nearby. "I take it that load of gold didn't get through to Colorado Springs What happened?"

Rose bit her lower lip, keeping her gaze straight ahead. Then she shrugged. "Papa had hired eight guards to haul it down the mountain. But Phil got to three of the guards be-fore they left, paid the three to kill the others. The three men and the gold are right up yonder. Foiled Papa's little ruse there, didn't we?" She laughed bitterly. "We're all heading for Haughton's hideout now, and soon we'll be a long, long ways from here."

Longarm remembered Yoakum riding through town yesterday. He'd no doubt just learned of Gandy's change of plans, and was heading for the guards. Longarm exhaled sharply through his nose. "They killed the other guards, I reckon. . . ."

"Blew 'em up with dynamite." Rose turned to Longarm, her eyes serious. "You think me a monster. I'm not. Just desperate. Besides, none of this was my doing. I just wanted away from my brutish father and his straps."

Longarm laughed. Lightning bolts of pain seared through both ears. He stopped and let his head hang slack against the stirrup fender.

Rose glowered at him, swerved her horse close. Her voice was sharp. "Don't get uppity or I'll let them kill you."

She gigged her horse up ahead of Yoakum. A few minutes later, Yoakum yelled into a dense pine thicket, "Stay with the gold! We'll be back after we've taken care of a little problem!"

Longarm's horse climbed a steep cut, threaded around gray rocks, and stopped. Yoakum appeared shortly to jerk Longarm off the horse by his collar. Longarm hit the ground on his shoulder, grunting as a thick wave of excruciating pain washed over him.

"Time to say good night, Deputy Long." Yoakum chuckled as he began dragging the lawman toward a hole gaping in a wall of crenelated rock. The hole was an old mine portal swathed in tailings. Coleridge grabbed Longarm's feet, and together he and Yoakum carried him over the tailings and set him down on the lip of the hole.

"Grab his other arm," Yoakum said. "We'll toss the son of a bitch—"

Longarm bolted off his knees, rammed his head into Yoakum's belly. Yoakum fell with a startled cry, hitting his own head on the rocks. Fighting back the pain and nausea, Longarm scuttled onto his knees and stretched both his tied hands toward the double-action Remington on Yoakum's left hip.

He'd wrapped his right hand around the revolver's butt

when Yoakum slammed his right fist into the side of Longarm's head. The lawman sagged backward over his heels, lights flashing, then gradually dimming as he felt a hand on his shoulder jerking him sideways and down, down, down . . . bouncing and rolling on riven rock before everything went black.

Yoakum gained his feet, wincing at the pain in his head, then slipped one of his revolvers from its holster and thumbed back the hammer. He aimed the pistol into the hole.

Rose's voice rose sharply behind him. "Phil, I said no more killing!"

Yoakum turned toward her. She stood holding her horse's reins at the base of the tailing pile.

"Rose, Goddamnit," exclaimed Coleridge standing six feet to Yoakum's right, "what the hell so pains you about killing this consarned lawman anyways? He's a threat to us, my flower!"

"I don't want him killed, that's all. He's different from the others."

"Doesn't make any goddamn sense, Rose," Yoakum said, breathing sharply. "I'm gonna kill him so we don't have to worry about him."

"If you do, Phil," Rose shouted, "I'll go back and tell Papa about the whole plan!"

Yoakum stood atop the tailing, his pistol in his hand, glaring down at her. Finally, he glanced at Coleridge, then cast his gaze into the pit, and holstered the Remington.

He cursed and started toward the horses lined out behind Rose. "What the hell. Cougar'll probably get him tonight anyway . . ."

As he approached the horses, Yoakum stuck two fingers in his mouth and whistled. When the three guards appeared from the dense forest, leading two mules carrying ironbanded strongboxes marked HOLY SMOKES MINE, LULU CITY, CO, Yoakum mounted his horse and rode over to meet the approaching riders.

They were big, beefy, bearded men in ratty clothes. Two carried double-barreled shotguns in thigh holsters, while the third, whose long, blond hair hung over the broad shoulders of his bear coat, wore bandoliers crisscrossed on his chest.

Yoakum had a few words with the men, then rode back to Rose and Coleridge. "What were you talking to them about?" Rose asked suspiciously.

"Nothing." Yoakum gigged his horse ahead of her and Coleridge. "All right, let's head out. I'd like to get to Haughton's hideout by nightfall."

Rose had ridden five minutes behind Yoakum, her betrothed riding to her right, when an explosion roared in the trees behind them, back toward the mine diggings.

Close on the heels of the blast sounded a shrill whoop. Rose turned to see one of Yoakum's three men gallop toward her. He held his hat on his head and whooped once more as he joined the other two killers riding drag.

"She done closed up tight as a schoolmarm's legs!" he shouted.

Her face hot with fury, Rose turned to Yoakum, who continued riding with his back to her. "I told you not to kill him!"

Yoakum half-turned and raised his left hand, palm up. "We didn't kill him. We just sealed the mine so he can't get out!"

He turned and gigged his horse into a trot, throwing his black-hatted head back on his shoulders, laughing.

"Rose, you're not gonna tell your pa a damn thing," Ebeneezer scoffed, wrinkling his nose and slitting his eyes. "You want his money as much as the rest of us, Miss Fancy Bloomers."

Rose pursed her lips and stared straight ahead. Her voice was taut and low. "Maybe so." She let out a heavy silent yawn. "But if you think I'm ever giving you another blow job, dear Ebeneezer, you're badly mistaken!"

Chapter 17

Longarm took a deep breath, and was rewarded with a throat full of dust and cordite. His choking thrust him back into consciousness. He opened his eyes, squinting against the stinging dust and smoke, and looked around.

He was at the bottom of a shallow digging. Mine rubble pressed down on his arms and legs. The floor sloped upward on his left, rising to a heap of more rubble sealing off the door—a jagged, sloping patch of black in the near-darkness.

He blinked and turned his head as his eyes swept the mine's walls. He could make out fissures, cracks, and the chips and breaks from picks and hammers.

If he was entirely sealed inside the mine, the darkness would be complete. Black as pitch. It was more like the gray of a late-summer dusk.

He lifted each shoulder in turn, shrugging off the rocks. Then he lifted his legs, tied at the ankles, throwing more rocks off his knees and thighs, wincing. He felt as though he'd been punched with brass knuckles all over his body.

If he hadn't heard the familiar, snakelike hiss of the lit dynamite fuse, and hadn't rolled deeper into the cave and then into a cleft in the wall, he'd have been buried under the bulk of the rubble up yonder.

He pushed himself to a sitting position, working his wrists against the rope and looking around. If light were penetrating the cave, then air was too, and there might be a way out.

But first things first.

He kicked the remaining rocks off his legs, spied a rock with a relatively sharp edge, and scuttled toward it. He draped his wrists over the rock and began sawing back and forth. Damn slow work, the rope's braids catching on the rock's pits and cracks.

Coughing the mine dust from his lungs, but heartened by the faint hint of fresh air penetrating from somewhere behind him, he kept working, his wrists cramping, then working through the cramps until the first braid tore, then the second, and the third, until the rope snapped and his wrists sprang free.

He reached down and clumsily untied the ropes binding his ankles, his hands numb from the pinched circulation. When he'd finally untied the knot, he sat for a moment as the blood ran back into his hands and feet—a sharp ache akin to having your near-frozen limbs wrapped in barbed wire.

His head still pounding, he crawled on his hands and knees toward the murky light source and fresh air.

The fetor of bat guano and coyote shit mixed with the smell of the cordite and dust as he made his way through the narrowing, rock-strewn fissure, its ceiling brushing the top of his head as he crawled. Several times he ducked under low-hanging knobs and slithered around stone thumbs jutting from the walls.

At one point he crawled over a broken, rusty-headed pick. An unseen rat screeched intermittently.

At last he reached the light. Or got as close to it as he could.

Resting on his knees, hands on his thighs, he peered at the rocks blocking his way from the light washing in from outside—probably through another hole the prospectors had dug, working the same vein from two different angles. Apparently, this end of the mine had collapsed.

He reached forward, removed a rock from the heaped rubble. It loosed those on top of it, and several fell as Longarm scooted back, cursing. He was liable to bring the whole mine down on top of him, but there was no other way out.

He carefully removed another rock, then another, working with strained patience until he'd cleared a gap to the outside.

After removing his coat, he wriggled through the gap, finally collapsing just outside the narrow opening, breathing hard, his sleeves torn, his entire body layered in dust and grit.

The caws of angry crows brought him back to full consciousness. He lifted his head, peered into a fir towering over him. Several boughs were filled with the angry, black birds.

"Don't mind me," Longarm grunted, climbing to his knees. "I was just leaving."

He turned, reached back into the mine opening for the coat he'd pulled along, one sleeve loosely tied around his ankle. He shrugged into it, then climbed to his feet and staggered down the tailing pile, glancing around dubiously. The golden morning light lanced his eyes.

Leaving the last of the tailings, he stumbled down the hill, weaving around trees and shrubs. When he came upon fresh horse apples and hoofprints, he stopped, followed the trail with his eyes, then continued ambling down the hill, looking around for his horse.

He hoped Yoakum hadn't taken it. If so, he'd have a long walk back to Lulu City. By the time he could return with reinforcements, the trail to Haughton's lair would be cold.

At the bottom of the pine- and boulder-studded ravine in which he'd spied Rose sucking Ebeneezer's cock, he found his hat still dented from Yoakum's rifle butt. Longarm brushed it off, snugged it on his head, and looked around.

Wondering if the buckskin would come to a whistle, he stuck two fingers in his mouth, and blew.

At length, hoof thuds rose down ravine, growing louder. The horse's low, inquiring nicker sounded.

"I'll be damned," Longarm said, watching the buckskin trot toward him, dipping its head beneath branches and turning around trees and boulders. "This is my lucky day!"

When he spied his Winchester still stowed in his saddle boot, and his spare .44 in his saddlebags, he threw his arms around the horse's neck and kissed its bristled cheek.

Then he mounted up and headed back toward Yoakum's trail and, if luck stayed with him, to Haughton's lair.

After three hours following game trails and fording snowmelt creeks, Phil Yoakum reined his black horse to a halt in the middle of an ancient riverbed strewn with sand and rocks. Behind him, Coleridge, Rose, and the three men from Gandy's mule train checked down their own mounts and followed Yoakum's gaze to the mountain looming ahead.

The ridge towered a good thousand feet above the river bottom, carpeted in sparse yellow brush, with occasional cedars and gray rocks scattered along the slope.

At the base of the mountain, straight ahead of Yoakum's party, a black, jagged-edged tunnel mouth appeared. Two men squatted amongst the brush and rocks above the tunnel, holding rifles across their chests as they canted their faces at Yoakum, returning his gaze.

Yoakum had tied a red neckerchief to the end of his rifle barrel. Now he raised the gun, waved it high above his head slowly.

One of the men squatting above the tunnel mouth placed his hat on the end of his own rifle barrel, and returned the wave. When he'd lowered the rifle and donned his hat, both him and his partner relaxing against the rocks they were perched on, Yoakum turned to the girl and the men behind him.

"This is it, kids. Home sweet home."

Rose sighed. "Why do I feel like I'm being led into the devil's den?"

Yoakum squinted his one good eye at her. "There's no turning back now. You start having second thoughts, we'll have to kill you."

Rose bunched her lips and narrowed her brown eyes beneath the brim of her prim straw hat. "Do I look like I'm having second thoughts? I'm just hoping there's not going to be any double-crossing. I know how thieves work. If you had a hundred dollars, you'd steal a penny's worth of rock candy from a toddler."

"You've been reading Dead-Eye Dick's novels again, Miss Rose," Yoakum clucked as he edged his horse closer to hers. "And what the fuck do you think *you* are?" Suddenly, his right hand shot up, the knuckles smashing against Rose's right cheek.

She shrieked as her head snapped sideways. Covering that side of her face with a gloved hand, she shot an enraged glance at Yoakum. "Bastard!"

"I don't like bein' talked to in that fashion!" Yoakum rose high in his saddle. "Never have. And now that we're not all dancing to your pappy's fiddle anymore, I don't have to. You're on my turf now, you fucking little bitch!"

To his right, there was the unmistakable click of a gun hammer.

He turned to see Ebeneezer Coleridge glaring at him over the pocket pistol cocked in his right hand. The sun winked off the young man's glasses, so Yoakum couldn't see his eyes, but Coleridge's fair cheeks were pink with anger.

"Do that again, I'll kill you."

Behind Coleridge, the three well-armed mule skinners

cursed impatiently, sharing incredulous glances. Yoakum returned his own gaze to Coleridge.

"Eb, you and I both know that if you shoot *me*, my cousin and his men will kill you *and* Rose." He chuckled. "Who the hell do you think you're fucking with?"

With that, Yoakum turned in his saddle and booted the black forward, the hooves clomping along the rocky riverbed.

The others followed in a shaggy line—Rose and Ebeneezer conferring in hushed, angry tones—and soon they were in the tunnel that the ancient river had long since cut through the mountain's sandstone wall.

Steel-shod hooves and the squawk of leather echoed off the tunnel's jagged walls streaked with mineral deposits and pocked with the hivelike nests of cliff swallows.

The tunnel was seventy yards long. When the group emerged from the other end, Yoakum led them into a valley, over two low rises, and into the broad canyon on the other side, where a handful of wooden shacks nestled under the opposite ridge.

A tall stamping mill, missing as many boards from its frame as those remaining, stood near a massive log-and-sandstone building sprouting two smoke-blackened chimneys from each end.

The ridge above the buildings was honeycombed with the vague outlines of old wagon trails weaving around gaping mine portals and tailings, sun-bleached and grown up with weeds and capped with old snow. Large planks had been planted about six feet apart along the slope, each bearing a faded red letter to compose the words: LONE PINE MINING COMPANY.

Men in ragged trail garb—several wearing pieces of old Confederate uniforms—milled about two large cook fires fronting the mine's main office building, which was built up against the hill, its porch on seven-foot stilts. The men stopped milling to watch Yoakum's procession approach the cabin.

The thick wood smoke was rife with the smell of roasting meat and coffee. The smell of unwashed bodies and overfilled latrines was strong enough to bring tears to the eyes, but Yoakum didn't mind. To him, that was the smell of riches and freedom.

"Well, look what the cat dragged in," said a tall, dirty hombre standing near one of the fires. Squinting and listing to one side, as though drunk, he spread his lips back to reveal two gold front teeth. One hand fingered the walnut grips of his holstered .44.

"Ephraim, how you been?" Yoakam asked.

The man only glowered at him.

On the porch of the long, narrow cabin flanking the fires, Hawk Haughton climbed heavily up from a bench to rest his fists on the peeled-pine rail. He wore no hat, and his round, bald head fairly glistened in the high-country light.

"Was expectin' you last night, Phil." Haughton's voice was taut.

Grinning like the cat who ate the canary, Yoakum beckoned to his cousin. "Get down here, you old reprobate!"

Haughton's watery gray eyes roamed across the newcomers, working the chew snugged between his cheek and lower gum. Finally, he spat over the rail, wiped his mouth with the back of his hand, and moved down the steep stairs dropping from the stilted porch to the canyon floor, his spurs chinging, boots thumping, his open buffalo coat flapping around the two pearl-butted pistols on his hips.

The two men he'd been sitting with grabbed their rifles from against the cabin wall, and followed him down. The three moseyed stiffly toward Yoakum, drew up before his horse, the two with rifles flanking the outlaw leader. The silver loops hanging from Haughton's ears winked in the sunlight.

He squinted and canted his head to the right. "We had us a dry run yesterday, Phil. The train was carryin' two strongboxes filled with lead. You was supposed to make sure that didn't happen. That's why I always kept Nester and Dodge so close to town—so you could tell 'em the plan."

"Couldn't be helped," Yoakum said, holding up his right hand, palm out, as though pledging his allegiance. "The old bastard got a burr up his ass, decided to take the gold down the mountain by mule train." He half-turned, glancing at the three horseback riders surrounding the two pack mules. The men were slumped in their saddles, hungrily eyeing the deer roasting on one of the fires.

"Have a look for yourself," Yoakum invited Haughton.

The outlaw leader glanced skeptically up at Yoakum. He turned to his brother, Ephraim, then hitched his cartridge belts higher on his broad, womanish hips, rubbed his hand once more across his mouth, and sauntered over to the first of the two mules. He stared at the lockbox, a grin pulling at the corners of his thin mouth.

He glanced at Yoakum, who'd dismounted from the black and moved toward him. "If you got the gold in there, I'm gonna shit my britches!"

Yoakum sidled up to Haughton, shucked a big bowie knife from a sheath hanging down his back, and cut one of the crisscrossing ropes securing the box to the packsaddle. "Hope you got plenty of clean underwear, cousin," Yoakum said, cutting the other rope.

He nodded at two of the mounted guards. They both dismounted, came over, grabbed a hold of the box, eased it off the packsaddle and down to the ground between Haughton and Yoakum.

Yoakum crouched down, jerked the open padlock off the hasp, and drew the lid up and back, revealing fifteen gold bars stacked neatly within. They glowed more brightly than the westering sun.

Haughton shuffled back, as if the box were filled with diamondbacks, and shook his head. "I'll be God-fucking-damned." He looked up at Yoakum, his awe plain in his washed-out eyes.

Looking down at the gold, Ephraim said, "How in the fuck did you manage this . . . all on your own?"

Yoakum smiled at his cousins. "I'd like to take full credit, but the whelp up there next to his little flower petal was the one who wrestled the information out of old Gandy."

Ebeneezer Coleridge's cheeks colored with pride. "I could tell by the bullion man's behavior, something was amiss. I prodded the old fart just a little—without him realizing I was prodding, of course—and he spilled the proverbial beans. Only the bullion man, old Gandy himself, and the guards were supposed to know."

The youngster cast an injured glance at Rose sitting her horse beside his. "Didn't even trust me—his mine superintendent . . . his daughter's betrothed. . . ."

"Don't fret, Eb," Rose said, reaching over and placing a hand on Coleridge's cheek. "We'll soon be a thousand miles from the old son of a bitch!"

Haughton scowled at the pair, then turned to Yoakum. "Gandy's daughter?"

Yoakum nodded, turning the corners of his mouth down. "The Fancy Dan is her future husband. As per our agreement, they've been promised fifty thousand apiece plus safe passage to a spur line. They're on their own after that."

Haughton chuffed with disgust, then tipped his head toward Gandy's gold guards, two of whom stood to his right while the third still sat his horse, staring wide-eyed down at the strongbox, mesmerized.

"What about them?" Haughton asked Yoakum.

"I promised them each a thousand dollars."

"That's too much." Haughton had already drawn his pistols. Now he snapped back the triggers, shoved each barrel into the bellies of the two men before him.

Before the guards could do more than drop their jaws, Haughton's revolvers blasted. The men screamed, one staggering backward while the other dropped to his knees, trying to grab one of his holstered shotguns. Haughton shot him through the forehead, then turned both pistols on the man sitting the horse.

The horse had started at the pistol fire. The guard, not yet able to comprehend what had just happened to his partners, sawed back on the reins and gaped down at Haughton.

"Wha . . . ?" he cried as Hawk Haughton fired both revolvers at once while Ephraim hopped around on one foot, whooping like a crazed coyote.

The bullets punched the man off the horse. He hit the ground, rolled onto his belly, dust puffing around him, and lay still. The horse screamed and galloped away.

Hawk Haughton stared at the nearest dead man, balling his cheeks as powder smoke wafted around him. "I can understand cutting in Fancy Dan and his wench. Without them, this whole thing wouldn't have been possible."

He grinned up at Coleridge and Rose, both staring horrifically down at him, clutching their shying horses' reins against their chests.

"But we can't cut in everybody that turns us a friendly face," Haughton continued, returning his gaze to Yoakum.

Yoakum crouched over one of the men Haughton had shot. The man lay on his belly, groaning softly while moving one leg. Yoakum drew the man's pistol and inspected it closely, fiddling with the hammer. Then he aimed at the back of the wounded man's head, and fired.

He nodded as the guard gave a last jerk and lay still. "Those were pretty much my sentiments too, cousin."

Ephraim hooted and clapped his hands, gold teeth glinting, long hair whipping around his head.

When Hawk had ordered several men standing around the fire to haul the gold over to the smelter for reprocessing, he clamped a fat arm around his cousin's shoulders. "Come on up to the office, Phil, for a celebratory libation. We'll be entertaining important guests from Denver tonight. Tomorrow, we start for Mexico!"

Chapter 18

Longarm hunkered down in a bed of dead arctic aster and creeping juniper, and trained his field glasses over the lip of a rocky knoll. Peering straight west along the ancient riverbed curling around the knoll's base, he tightened the focus until Yoakum, Rose, Coleridge, and the three gold guards materialized before him.

Yoakum was waving a red neckerchief tied to the end of his rifle barrel while the others waited behind him, staring above the mouth of the tunnel, which the river had obviously gouged from the base of the fawn mountain. At first, Longarm wasn't sure whom the man was signaling; then he saw the rifle wave back at him.

Readjusting the glasses, he brought the two men out of the mountain, crouched amongst the gray rocks and spindly shrubs and holding rifles across their chests.

A quirley angled from the thin lips of the man on the right, who wore a leather-billed, butternut-gray forage hat and gray trousers partially concealed by a long wolf coat.

When Yoakum and the other riders rode into the tunnel, Longarm chewed his lip as he studied the two men on the mountain.

There was no way to sneak into the tunnel without the

sentinels spying him and possibly alerting the main camp. He could cross the mountain, but it would take too much time. The smartest thing to do would be to hightail it back to Lulu City and cable Billy Vail for help, but by the time supposed help arrived, Haughton, Yoakum, and all the others would be long gone with the Holy Smokes gold.

Again, Longarm swept the face of the mountain with the field glasses. Certain that only two men guarded the tunnel—Haughton must have been damn confident no one would ever follow him here—Longarm scuttled back off the knoll.

He returned to his horse tied in a spruce grove, dropped the field glasses into his saddlebags, shucked his Winchester, and began striding straight west along a shallow cut. Keeping a long, rocky, larch-stippled scarp between him and the mountain, he paralleled the mountain's base for about a hundred yards, then scampered over the scarp, traversed a grassy, snow-spotted bench, dodging between junipers and cedars, then scrambled straight up the mountain wall.

He used shrubs to help pull him along the slippery incline while casting cautious glances to his right, where the two guards lounged unseen above the tunnel mouth.

Fifty yards above the mountain's base, he moved east along the ridge, following a narrow game trail while keying on the rocky riverbed below. When he was nearly directly above the bed, but could not see the two guards amongst the shrubs and rocks, he dropped to one knee.

He needed to get lower, close enough to the tunnel mouth that he could see both guards clearly.

He'd begun sidestepping down the slope when a voice and footfalls rose. ". . . why he stuck me up here with a clabberhead such as you, I got no idea. Leave those cards alone. I'll be right back, you damn four-flusher."

A voice replied, but Longarm was too far away to pick up the words.

Sandy hair and a blue bandanna appeared above the

shoulder of the slope, bobbing above the bending yellow grass and strewn boulders. The man was heading up the slope toward Longarm. Heart thudding, the lawman dropped behind a low rock shaped like a plowshare, curling his legs beneath him and pressing his back flat against the ground.

Boots crunched grass nearby, and a long shadow slid over the boulder, darkening the creeping junipers to Longarm's right. The footsteps ceased. A man grunted, snorted caustically. There was the jingle of a belt being unbuckled, the thump of pistols and a cartridge belt falling to the ground.

As the man's piss began splashing the weeds, Longarm noticed that the brim of his own hat protruded an inch or so above the plowshare-shaped boulder he lay behind. He pressed his back down flatter, his right hand sliding out away from him, closing over a stone.

The piss stream stopped abruptly. The man's voice came, low but sharp, pitched with suspicion. "Hey . . ."

Longarm shot up to his knees, lifting the stone. The sandy-haired man with the blue bandana faced Longarm, his pale dong hanging out the open fly of his worn duck pants, eyes wide, mouth agape.

Longarm cocked his arm and loosed the rock as the sandy-haired gent stiffened and began lurching straight back, stretching his mouth to scream. The rock bounced off the man's forehead just above the bridge of his nose. As the rock fell at his feet, the man stumbled back and sideways, grunting. He clapped his left hand to his head.

"Son of a *bitch*!"

Longarm spewed a couple of heartfelt curses of his own as the man, instead of being knocked unconscious, dropped to his knees and reached for one of the two pistols holstered on his cartridge belt. Longarm raised his rifle, quickly ramming a shell into the breech, and drilled a round through the man's chest.

The man screamed. Triggering his revolver into the air, he flew backward.

Longarm rammed another shell into his Winchester's breech as the sound of running footfalls sounded from downslope. Labored breaths raked, and Longarm had no sooner extended his rifle in the direction of the riverbed than the other guard appeared, holding his rifle high across his chest.

The visor on the guard's ancient Confederate forage cap lifted as he peered uphill. The man stopped as his blue eyes flashed in the sunlight.

He snapped the rifle toward his cheek, but the stock didn't reach his chin before Longarm's forty-four round had punched him straight back down the slope. Wolf coat flapping around his thighs, he hit a rock, bounced, and rolled into a brush-choked cleft between two boulders.

Longarm ejected the spent shell, levered a fresh one into the chamber, and looked around. He listened hard for a long time, wondering if anyone else had heard the shots.

When he'd stood there for several minutes, hearing nothing but the breeze and the distant screech of a hawk, he leaned over the man with the blue bandanna, whose eyes stared up death-glazed.

Glancing once more around the mountain, he hop-scotched rocks to the base of the slope. He leaped off the last rock to the riverbed, moved left to the mouth of the tunnel, and edged a look inside.

Only deep shadows set against the lighted oval of the tunnel's other end, birds arcing in and out of the distant daylight. The breeze whistling through the tunnel was cold and dank.

Longarm returned to his horse tied in the spruces, slid his rifle into the saddle boot, and swung into the leather.

He booted the horse back into the riverbed and entered the tunnel, the horse's clacking hooves echoing around him. The tunnel was about fifty yards long and choked with rocks and driftwood from the last gully-washer. In the middle, it was as dark as a well, but grew gradually lighter as he approached the other end.

A few feet from the other side, he stopped and looked around, his rifle in his hands, his heart thudding. He'd half-expected to find himself in Haughton's encampment, but there was nothing here but scarps and twisted trees and strewn rocks.

Before him, the riverbed narrowed between high sandstone walls capped with stunted, high-country firs and spruces. The walls of the cut shone with fossilized tree roots and chips of animal bones.

Longarm remained at the tunnel's edge for several minutes, looking around and listening. Relatively certain that this end of the tunnel wasn't being watched, he followed the hoof-pocked riverbed eastward for half a mile, turned into a narrower dry wash still choked with dirty snow, where crows and magpies feasted on the decomposed carcass of a fawn, and continued past an old mine drift.

As the walls of the wash lowered, Longarm heard voices. Immediately, he turned the horse back the way he'd come.

After twenty yards, he dismounted, shucked his rifle, and ran forward. He dropped behind a natural levee and, doffing his hat and keeping his head low, stared north across the canyon.

Buildings were spread out along the base of the far ridge. Large planks stood out against the slope, high above the buildings, their faded red letters announcing: LONE PINE MINING COMPANY.

The far side of the canyon was awash in blue wood smoke. Men and horses milled around two fires. More men sat around the raised porch of what Longarm assumed was the mine's main office building, built high against the far slope and shaded by tall pines and balsam firs.

"Here we are," Longarm said, adjusting his grip on the rifle.

He didn't like working with anyone else. But now, as he glanced around the dozen or so men gathered a hundred yards away, and chewed his mustache, he wished he had a whole platoon of bluebellies and a Gatling gun.

* * *

Two hours later, the sky had turned violet, and cold, purple shadows had spilled down the mountains.

Longarm stood atop the ridge behind the mine, staring down the steep slope past the old portals and tailing piles and weeded-over wagon trails at the dark roofs of the mine camp buildings.

Leaving his horse hidden in the canyon and making his way up the ridge from the canyon's eastern end, well out of view of Haughton's men, the lawman had had plenty of time to chew over the outlaws' setup.

They'd obviously taken over the Lone Pine Mine works, which had been shut down three years ago by its owners, three prominent Denver businessmen, and were using the canyon for a hideout. They were probably using the old smelter and bullion room to melt Gandy's Holy Smokes gold, pour it into fresh molds, and give it a phony stamp. Most likely, they'd even concocted phony legal documents validating the stamp so they could then sell the gold as their own at the Denver mint.

A slick operation for crazy old Rebels from out Appalachia way . . .

Longarm knew his chances of arresting any of these men were slim to nil. But before the light had gone, he'd spotted several heavy wagons parked near the mine office. They intended to ship the gold soon. If he knew for sure that they were heading for Denver, Longarm could simply wire Billy Vail and have the chief marshal waiting for them with a contingent of deputies and soldiers.

But if they were heading somewhere other than Denver, it might be a long time, if ever, before Solomon Gandy saw his gold again.

He could hear Billy Vail in his ear: "You decided you'd do *what?* I told you to just *locate* the hideout then wire me for *backup!*"

Chuffing dryly and wishing he had a shot of rye to brace him, Longarm began moving slowly down the ridge. Holding the rifle across his chest, he weaved between rotting slash piles and ore and rock mounds, crossing the switch-backing wagon trails and occasionally slipping on strewn talus or icy snowdrifts.

His breath puffed before him. In the silent mountain night, his boots clicked loudly on the rocks or snapped branches. As he moved farther down the mountain, the din of celebratory voices grew louder, as did the jubilant strains of a fiddle, covering the noise of his own movements.

He'd reckoned on the main office building, and now he stepped down the slope directly behind the building, its corrugated tin roof glittering with reflected starlight. The voices grew louder, as did the smell of tobacco and roasting meat and corn mash.

As Longarm pressed his back against the wall, he heard glasses clink together. Jubilant whoops rose in the building behind him, for a moment drowning the fiddle.

He sidled up to a window, removed his hat, and peered into the building. A half-dozen or so men had gathered there. He recognized Hawk Haughton from the description Billy had provided—a big, fat, greasy man, bald as a skinned chicken, adorned with jewelry. He wore at least six rings on his pudgy, white hands, and silver rings jostled from his stretched earlobes.

His brother, the gold-toothed, long-haired Ephraim, sat to his right, nodding his head to the music and stomping one foot.

Longarm also recognized three of Haughton's top lieu-tenants. But the men who caught his eye and held it for an inordinate time were the three sitting directly across the long pine table from Haughton, a bottle of brandy on the table before them, heavy goblets in their hands or rising to lips mantled with carefully trimmed mustaches, framed by stylish beards.

Longarm's heart gave a jerk as he stared at three of Denver's most prominent businessmen—Stanley McDon-ald, Thomas Blackburn, and Miles Solte. They'd been the primary stockholders in the Lone Pine Mine, when the mine was up and running. Longarm had heard they'd taken a loss when the veins in the canyon had pinched out, and their Denver-based businesses had suffered.

Apparently, they'd found a way to retrieve their losses, not the least of which was throwing in with Haughton's men, reopening their smelter to reprocess the stolen gold, and—Longarm stared at the portmanteau sitting open on the lap of one of Haughton's men, who was apparently counting the money bundled and heaped inside—buying the very gold they'd reprocessed.

Most likely, the wagons Longarm had seen parked in the yard earlier belonged to the businessmen. They'd arrived to haul Haughton's stash to the mint, no doubt telling anyone interested that they'd reopened their own mine.

The mine was remote enough that no one was likely to check their story.

When Haughton suddenly turned toward him, raising his glass in another toast, Longarm ducked back behind the wall.

"And here's to good whiskey!" Haughton shouted. "You boys know how long we've been drinkin' the witches brew Ephraim's been mixin' in his tubs?"

"Far too long, I daresay," replied one of the businessmen, the strong Eastern accent identifying Blackburn, whom Longarm had once shared a theater box with. The man had a fat wife, three dull, pampered daughters, and a sprawling house not far from that of Cynthia Larimer's uncle.

Longarm had heard he'd been a pimp before coming West and opening two saloons and a carriage factory.

Longarm took one more glance at the portmanteau. The man counting the money grinned wide, showing small, brown teeth, and kept shaking his head with utter awe and disbelief at the fortune before him.

While the Haughtons and the businessmen clinked glasses and toasted their health, the fiddle player paused to cough and spit into a sandbox. From somewhere to Longarm's right, Rose's voice cried out beseechingly.

Longarm ducked under the window, moved to the end of the building, and edged a look toward the yard and the open canyon.

A couple of men stood near one of the burned-down fires, smoking and talking, their backs to Longarm.

The lawman drew back, holding the rifle straight up and down in his hands. Drawing a deep breath, he bolted across the open ground, heading for the shack from which Rose's feeble cries issued.

Chapter 19

Longarm wove through the pines and pressed his back against the rear wall of the building just north of the mine office. The whipsawed boards were warm from stoves ticking behind the thin wall, the sounds half drowned by men's laughter, the ratcheting of shuffled cards, and the low groans and feeble curses of a girl somewhere at the far right end of the shack.

There was a back door, and on each side of the door, a window. Longarm stole over to the window left of the door, removed his hat, and peeked inside.

The glass was warped and smoke-streaked, but he could see seven men sitting at one of three small tables surrounded by bunks. They were playing poker. Ebeneezer Coleridge was one of the players. His pinched expression and nervous eyes behind his glinting spectacles told Longarm that the young man didn't like how things were going.

"It isn't right, it just isn't right," Coleridge said, shaking his head as sweat rolled down his cheeks. "Playing for the honor of my wife is a horror I didn't expect to experience even amongst cutthroats such as yourselves."

The six rough-hewn, unshaven men around him laughed and sucked their cigarettes and cigars. One man, tipping back a whiskey bottle, brought it down suddenly, spraying the liquid on the coins and paper money piled in the middle of the table.

"Jackson, you goddamn pig!" exclaimed one of the other outlaws, scowling at the damp money with disgust.

"I can't help that Fancy Dan here made me laugh!"

The argument continued as Longarm, looking around the room and not seeing Rose, only hearing her muffled complaints, ducked beneath the window, stole past the door, and paused beside the second window six feet from the end of the long building. Holding his hat in one hand, the rifle in the other, he peered around the window's left edge.

Rose lay on her back, on one of the several bunks lined up against the walls, her corset and chamise torn. One of the outlaws—a slender gent with long, dirty gray hair and a shaggy black beard—lay on the far side of the cot, propped on an elbow and running the barrel of his pistol up and down between her breasts.

Rose shook her head and begged the man not to hurt her. He merely laughed and continued running his revolver barrel up and down the valley between her pert, pink-tipped orbs, occasionally stopping to press the bore against her chin.

"Pow!" he guffawed. "How'd you like that?"

"Please, don't!" Rose begged, tears rolling down her cheeks.

"I reckon we're just gonna have to see if your Mister—" He stopped and frowned. "What was your beau's name again?"

"Ebeneezer," Rose sniffed.

"If your Mr. Ebeneezer can win you back from ole Mose and the boys. If not, I reckon you're gonna get to know me and the boys real well!" His face, which was long and horsey, suddenly sobered. "But don't you worry none. I for one will be very gentle with ya."

The man guffawed again, and Rose said something else,

but Longarm had already doffed his hat and walked to the end of the building. He didn't know why—maybe it was their time on the train or that she hadn't wanted him killed—but he wanted get Rose out of there.

But how?

He stopped and looked around at the several other wood or stone structures scattered willy-nilly amongst the pines and spruces, abandoned wagons, tipples and other mining equipment, deep-gouged wagon tracks, and dilapidated corrals.

No men seemed to be out and about this end of the camp. Jogging between pines, Longarm investigated the other buildings, looking for a dynamite cache. There had to be one around here somewhere, probably a good distance from the occupied buildings and the smelter and retort room, where a stray spark might ignite it.

If he could distract the men in the bunkhouse, he might be able to get Rose to safety. Then he could go after the others.

When he came to an isolated log stable with an attached corral, he opened the doors facing the far side of the canyon, and stepped inside.

The usual barn odors assaulted him, as did total darkness. Holding his hands out, Longarm found a lamp hanging on a joist, and lit it. Raising the lamp high, he discovered over a dozen horses and mules stalled around him, molasses-black eyes gleaming through the shadows.

None of the stock seemed to mind his presence overmuch—one gave only a low, inquisitive nicker and nudged its grain sack off the stall partition. Longarm walked amongst the animals, shielding the lamp cylinder with his hand so the glow wouldn't be seen from outside.

He was walking along the barn's right rear corner when he discovered a wooden trapdoor four feet long by three feet wide, bearing three steel hinges and a steel lift ring. Judging by the lack of hay and dust over it, the door had recently been opened.

Setting his rifle aside, he held the lamp with one hand

and pulled the lift ring with the other. The door popped up with a raspy scrape, and Longarm set it back against the floor as the smell of cool earth, mold, and gunpowder wafted over his face.

Things were looking up. With dynamite, he had a chance, however slim.

He set the lamp beside the hole, then started down a rough wooden ladder, which creaked beneath his weight. He grabbed the lantern and continued six feet down to the earthen bottom of the pit, and swung the lamp around.

Five minutes after he'd descended the hole, Longarm climbed out again, the heads of several dynamite sticks— to which he'd attached the caps and fuses—protruding from his two big coat pockets.

He closed the door quietly, blew out the lamp, moved back through the barn's open doors, and retraced his steps, moving faster now, his pulse throbbing, to the long bunkhouse where Ebeneezer Coleridge was trying to win his wife back in the poker game.

Longarm didn't slow his pace as he ran past the bunkhouse's lighted windows, but from Rose's loud screams and curses, he figured that Ebeneezer had lost the game.

"You lay down with dogs, Miss Rose," Longarm muttered as he jogged past the open space between buildings, "you wake up with fleas."

He crouched beside the back door of the office, his right foot on one of the three wooden steps. Fishing two sticks of dynamite out of his coat pockets, he held the sticks in one hand, snapped a match to life with the other. When the flame was burning, he touched it to both fuses, dropped the match, and stared at the sizzling sparks trailing toward the dynamite sticks.

When the fuses had burned down two inches, he jerked open the office's back door, and stepped inside. All faces turned toward him, including that of the fiddle player, who dragged his bow raucously across the fiddle strings, brows beetled with befuddlement.

Longarm stood tall in the doorway, feet spread, a dynamite stick sizzling in each hand. By law, he was obliged to give criminals a chance to drop their weapons before he could sling lead or anything else at them. Longarm wasn't sure if that held true when said lawman was outgunned twenty to one, but let no one say he didn't always dot his i's and cross his t's.

"Gentleman, I'm the law. You gonna give yourselves up and come peaceful?"

All at once, the outlaws, including the Denver men, jerked their hands to their holsters or rifles. Phil Yoakum reached for a sawed-off shotgun, bellowing, *"Fuck!"*

"Didn't think so."

Longarm tossed one stick under the table at which Haughton and the businessmen were sitting, and one to the man sitting on the cot beside the money-filled portmanteau. While Haughton bellowed and slid his chair back from the table, the man on the cot grabbed the stick out of the air and held it before his face, staring at it, his lower jaw hanging, terror-stricken sounds rising from his throat.

Longarm bolted straight back, slammed the door, and leaped onto the slope behind the office. He ducked down behind a pine bole as the men screamed and scrambled around inside the office, someone triggering a pistol, two slugs plowing through the closed door.

The first stick ignited with a muffled roar.

The second followed a half-wink later, clipping the rising scream of the man on the cot, blowing out a window, and blasting the door open. As men screamed shrilly and smoke puffed through the windows and door, orange flames and shadows leaped around inside.

Longarm bolted out from behind the tree bole as shouts and yells rose from the far side of the bunkhouse, boots pounding the floorboards.

When he was directly behind the bunkhouse, Longarm dropped to one knee. He could hear men bolting out the front, spurs chinging and rifle levers rasping. When no one came out the back, he rushed down the slope, careening off trees, and ripped open the back door.

Inside, Ebeneezer Coleridge sat on the floor, his back against the front wall. His legs were spread before him, hands hanging limp between his thighs. His face was blood-smeared, both eyes swollen nearly shut. His hair was mussed and filthy, his shirt torn. His glasses lay smashed on the floor beside the gambling table.

He stared at Longarm, his ruined face expressionless.

To Longarm's right, Rose groaned and sobbed. The lawman looked down the aisle between the bunks. The girl lay facedown on the floor in the middle of the aisle, her torn dress bunched around her thighs.

Outside, men shouted and boots pounded the hard-packed yard. The smell of burning wood filled the air.

A deep, angry voice rose above the others. *"Find him!"*

Longarm swore and ran over to Rose, crouched down, leaned his rifle against a bunk, and threw her over his shoulder. "No more penny dreadfuls for you, Miss Rose."

Grabbing his rifle, he ran back to the main part of the room.

He stopped and looked down at Coleridge while he lit a cigar, balancing the half-conscious Rose on his shoulder. "Sorry, junior, but you're on your own."

The kid was so beat up, he just sat and stared. Longarm almost felt sorry for him.

Hearing voices and running footfalls from over near the cabin he'd just blown up, and from which the smell of smoke grew thicker, he stepped to the door and looked out. Three men were running past the bunkhouse, rifles in their hands, angry glints in their eyes. One looked at Longarm, looked away, turned back to him, and stopped.

"Hey!"

Longarm had plucked a dynamite stick from his coat pocket. Now, he calmly touched the fuse to his cigar. As the three outlaws began swinging their rifles up, Longarm slung the dynamite stick at their feet.

One of the outlaws bellowed, "Look out!"

They'd leapt only two or three feet away before the stick exploded, the cherry-red globe of fire kicking up dust and manure as it tranformed to sparks and sifting white smoke. One of the men lay slumped, his clothes burning.

Longarm didn't bother checking out the other two. He hefted Rose higher on his shoulder and bolted across the yard, angling toward the stone building with a massive chimney, which had probably been a blacksmith shop for keeping the mine wagons rolling.

Halfway across the yard, he glanced to his left and behind. The mine office building was fully engulfed. A couple of men were slumped on the ground before it. Hawk Haughton was rolling in the dirt trying to snuff the flames licking at his back. Phil Yoakum was down on all fours, his clothes and face fire-blackened, his eye patch turned toward Longarm.

His voice broke as he yelled, "Get that son of a bitch *now*!"

Two of the other gang members had already spotted Longarm. One ran toward him, raising a pistol, as another dropped to one knee snugging his rifle to his shoulder.

As the pistol and the rifle cracked simultaneously, the slugs kicking up dust and weeds at Longarm's boots, the lawman took his rifle in his right hand. Leaning to one side to keep Rose on his right shoulder, he plucked another dynamite stick from his coat pocket with his left hand, lit it, and tossed it.

Grabbing his rifle by the barrel stock, he bounded forward once more.

The dynamite blew. One of the shooters screamed. There was the thud and clatter of a body and a rifle hitting the ground.

More guns popped, Yoakum bellowing like a poleaxed mule as Longarm ducked behind the blacksmith shop.

Quickly Longarm set Rose down at the base of the blacksmith's rear wall. He hefted his rifle in both hands, rammed a shell into the breech, and ran around the building toward the burning office.

Silhouetted against the fire, several men ran toward him, pistols or rifles glinting in the firelight. Longarm stopped near the front of the blacksmith shop, and extended the rifle straight out from his right hip.

He fired, levered, fired again, slinging lead across the yard.

One outlaw did a bizarre dance to his left and dropped, throwing his rifle over his head. At nearly the same time, two more went down, screaming, one triggering a pistol into his own left foot. One dove behind a stock tank. As he lifted his head and rifle over the top of the tank, the rifle barrel flashing firelight, Longarm fired two more quick shots.

The man groaned and threw his head back before falling straight back against a well coping.

Ejecting the smoking shell from his rifle breech, Longarm crouched and whipped his gaze right and left and back again. He was expecting another shot. None came. Nothing moved except the flames churning up from the burning office and the smoke boiling up toward the stars.

Frozen there, Longarm automatically thumbed fresh shells into the rifle's loading gate. He kept his eyes on the yard and burning cabin, sweeping his gaze over the bodies humped before him.

He'd slipped five shells into the rifle when a light flashed near one of the three wagons parked, tongues hanging, before the bunkhouse. A pistol popped. The bullet plowed through Longarm's right shoulder.

The shot felt like a blow from a bung starter, punching him off his feet. His back hit the ground hard, the Winchester flying above his head and landing with a clatter.

He glanced up at the rifle, tried to reach for it. His arm felt like a ton of aching lead. The arm wouldn't move.

Clutching the wound with his left hand, Longarm peered toward the wagon. A big man, his bald head and sil-

175

ver earrings reflecting umber firelight, lumbered out from behind the wagon and staggered toward Longarm.

Hawk Haughton held a pearl-gripped revolver in his left hand. His torn clothes were black and smoking. A bloody wound gaped in his left side. Holding his left hand over the wound, he walked heavy-footed toward Longarm, and raised the pistol.

"Fucking son of a bitch!" He triggered the pistol, and the slug spanged off a rock just left of Longarm's head.

The pitch of the gun's report told Longarm the weapon was a Colt .41, the "long Colt," whose cartridge was slightly longer than the .45. The additional length gave it more stopping power while compromising accuracy at greater distances. The man's first shot had been a lucky hit.

Pop!

Longarm winced as the next slug tore into the ground just beyond him. He stared as Haughton staggered toward him, stumbling as though his ankles were broken, his jacket still smoldering from the dynamite blast.

"You're gonna die, you bastard son of a ten-cent whore!" Haughton bellowed, his voice cracking as one knee nearly buckled.

Regaining his balance, he glanced around while thumbing the Colt's hammer back.

"How the fuck am I s'posed to start a revolution without any *men*?"

Longarm looked at his rifle. He tried to reach for it. No good. He couldn't get his right hand to do more than twitch.

Haughton extended the pistol straight out before him, aiming down the barrel. "Tell me *that*!" The revolver roared, the slug clipping the heel of Longarm's left boot.

Longarm moved his left hand to the grips of his .44 holstered on his left hip. Clumsily—he'd never been much good with his left hand—he slid the gun from the cross-draw holster, wrapped his fingers around the walnut grips, and grimaced as another lance of searing pain caromed through his wounded shoulder.

Haughton was ten feet away and closing, shuttling his crazy eyes between the burning mine office and Longarm stretched out in the shrubs beside the blacksmith shop. He stopped suddenly, swaying, and glared at Longarm, sweat streaking his charred face, white teeth showing between his spread lips.

Holding the pistol straight down at his side, he cocked it, his entire body jerking with the effort. *"What the fuck's your name?"*

"Deputy U.S. Marshal Custis Long," Longarm said, his voice pinched, as he raised the cocked .44.

He leveled the revolver at Haughton's chest, squinting his right eye. The outlaw leader's own eyes snapped wide.

Longarm steadied the revolver, pulled the trigger. The bullet punched through Haughton's chest, just left of his heart. The man stumbled backward.

"But you can call me Longarm."

Longarm fired again, placing another hole four inches right of the first. Haughton stumbled two more steps straight back and dropped to his knees.

He looked up, breathing hard, blood frothing on his lips.

As his enraged, glassy eyes met Longarm's, Longarm drilled a hole through the man's bulging forehead.

Haughton sagged backward on his heels, twitched, and lay still.

Longarm stared at the man for a moment, catching his breath as the powder smoke wafted around his face. Finally, he removed his neckerchief and shoved it into the bullet hole in his shoulder, cursing through gritted teeth as the night flickered around him, and he almost passed out.

Slowly, he pulled his legs beneath him and, holding his wounded arm across his belly, gained his feet. Holding the .44 straight down in his left hand, he ambled around the

177

yard, inspecting the burned, charred, or bullet-riddled bodies—seven or so. The others, including the Denver businessmen and Ephraim Hawk, had no doubt died in the mine office.

Longarm found Yoakum near a burning timber that had fallen from the mine office roof. The one-eyed outlaw lay on his left hip and shoulder, gritting his teeth, shivering and breathing sharply as his good eye stared up at the lawman with beseeching.

His pants were burned nearly off, revealing the charred skin of his legs. The dynamite blast had laid his left arm open, the sleeve of his Prince Albert coat hanging in tatters around it.

"Finish me, Goddamnit," he grated, teeth clattering.

Longarm chuffed and holstered his revolver. An ivory-gripped Remington lay near the outlaw. Longarm kicked it out of his reach, and turned away. "Not doing you any favors, you privy rat."

Longarm turned and, clutching his right wrist taut to his belly, walked around to the rear of the blacksmith shop. Rose sat where he'd left her, a black silhouette against the shop's stone wall.

Longarm crouched down and called her name.

She remained slumped against the wall, her chest still.

Longarm said her name once more, then saw a black smudge on the side of her neck, just below her right ear. He pulled her toward him, and her head flopped forward. Blood shone in her hair, dribbling down her left shoulder blade. Apparently, a bullet—most likely, a ricochet—had pierced her skull when Longarm had hauled her across the yard.

He leaned her back against the wall, and her chin dropped to her chest. "Rose, Rose, Rose." He folded her hands in her lap, closed her eyelids with his thumb and index finger, and straightened with a weary sigh.

Walking back toward the burning mine office, he

stopped suddenly. Hooves thudded—two riders coming fast from the east.

He waited there, pistol in his left hand, hammer cocked. Shit, now what?

The riders formed from the shadows, becoming the tall, thick form of Solomon Gandy in a cowhide, fleece-lined greatcoat and floppy-brimmed black hat. The sheriff from Lulu City, Hulbert Hooley, followed on a gray mare. He wore a red mackinaw and rabbit hat with ear flaps. The sheriff's five-pointed star winked in the starlight.

Longarm hadn't thought he'd ever be glad to see the pious old miner again, but he'd just started wondering how he was going to get out of here with his bullet-shattered shoulder from which he'd probably already lost a good quart of blood.

Gandy checked his horse down ten feet from Longarm. He held a double-barreled Greener across his saddle bows. "Longarm?"

The lawman just stared at him. Gandy and Hooley rode up to within a few feet. Gandy shuttled his curious gaze between Longarm and the fire and back again. He didn't say anything.

"She's dead, Gandy."

Gandy's voice was barely audible above the snaps and pops of the flames. "She in with 'em?"

Longarm nodded. "She's behind the blacksmith shop."

Gandy didn't even look at the building, but raised his voice above the flames' roar. "Where's my gold?"

Longarm stared at the man for a moment, seeing the sanctimonious old reprobate Rose had described. Feeling sorry for the girl, he gave a caustic grunt and said, "Bullion room, most likely."

"Heyah!" Gandy booted his horse into a gallop, racing into the shadows at the far end of the yard.

Hooley pulled up beside Longarm and cast his glance around the yard heaped with dead men. "You do all this?"

"I had help from a few sticks of dynamite. Yoakum's over yonder. You'll find Mr. Coleridge in the bunkhouse. He's about the only one you'll have to arrest." Longarm's head felt heavy. "How did you . . . ?"

"A couple of Mr. Gandy's miners saw Yoakum ride into the mountains, then Coleridge and Rose. Gandy fetched me to help track 'em." Staring at Longarm's shoulder, Hooley said, "You gonna make it?"

Longarm was already falling forward, throwing his left hand out toward the sheriff's horse. "I . . . just need to rest a bit." Longarm's hand slid off the mare's neck.

He was out before he hit the ground.

Epilogue

Longarm was only half-aware of being hauled by wagon back to Lulu City, then being half-led, half-carried upstairs to his room in the London Hotel.

When he was fully conscious again, four days later, his shoulder was sewn and bandaged, his right arm suspended in a sling made from what he assumed were women's discarded unmentionables.

The beautiful Zeena was spoon-feeding him, and it was from her that he learned that Gandy had hauled his gold back to the mine, then shipped it off—safely, this time—to the Denver mint.

Rose had been buried in Solomon Gandy's private cemetery, Gandy apparently telling no one of his daughter's involvement with the gold thieves. Ebeneezer Coleridge was locked up in the Lulu City jail.

Sheriff Hooley had cabled Billy Vail for the bedridden Longarm, informing the head marshal about what had transpired and that while Longarm was presently incapacitated, he'd no doubt be heading back to headquarters soon.

A week and a half into his recovery, Longarm and Zeena were frolicking doggie-style atop Longarm's bed in the early evening, when boots pounded the London's stairs. Zeena gasped, squeezing the brass spools at the head of the bed, throwing her head back on her shoulders, staring at the wall. Her hair was a swirling black mass across her back, glistening in the umber lamplight.

Kneeling behind her, his good hand clutching her left hip, Longarm stopped thrusting.

His swollen dong was buried in the woman's hot bowels as he cocked his head to listen to the footfalls coming along the hall.

"It's Sandy," Zeena whispered. "I'd know that shuffling gait anywhere."

Before Longarm could respond, a light knock sounded on the door.

"Deputy Long?" Sandy's voice, all right.

Frozen at the end of Longarm's shaft, Zeena stopped breathing.

Longarm said casually, "Yes, Sandy?"

"A reply from Marshal Vail in Denver, sir."

"Would you read it to me, Sandy?"

"Yessir." The sound of an envelope being torn open, the telegraph flimsy removed. Sandy's voice: "To Deputy U.S. Marshal Custis Long. Stop. You took down entire Haughton Gang by yourself? Stop. Bullshit. Stop. Cease your tomfoolery and file an official report. Stop. Will expect you in my office no later than Friday morning. End stop. Signed, Head Marshal, William H. Vail, Denver, Colorado."

"Well, that suspicious son of a bitch," Longarm groused.

Zeena turned her head to one side, gave an indignant grunt, and wagged her ass impatiently.

Longarm turned to the door. "Sandy, will you send a response to his response?"

Zeena groaned.

"Yessir."

"To Marshal Billy Vail, Denver office, etc. Still recovering from wounds incurred during Haughton Gang dustup. Need at least another full week to recover. Will return by

Friday after next with prisoner in tow. Your noble servant, Custis Long, etc., etc."

There was a hollow scratching sound, as if Sandy were writing out the note against the door. "I'll send it right off, Marshal."

"If Billy replies again, save it for tomorrow, will you, Sandy? I'm feeling right fatigued. I reckon I'll sleep the rest of the night."

"Anything I can get for you, sir?"

"That'll be all."

Silence. Longarm turned his head forward and was about to do something about his wilting member when, on the other side of the door, Sandy cleared his throat.

"Deputy Long?"

Longarm chuffed and turned back to the door. "What is it, Sandy?"

"Would you ask Ma what she'd like me to do with that side of venison Rupert Clarke brought in from his hunting trip?"

Zeena gasped with horror, bolted away from Longarm, and curled up against the brass headboard, knees to her chest, arms around her knees.

Sandy continued. "Shall I cut off a portion for tomorrow's stew and store the rest in the cellar, or does she prefer it prepared in some other fashion?"

Zeena stared wide-eyed at Longarm, her face ashen. "Oh, my God!" she mouthed, wriggling her toes.

Staring down at her, Longarm shrugged his good shoulder.

Again, Sandy cleared his throat. Quietly, he said, "Uh, please tell Ma it's no never mind to me what she does in her spare time. Since she ignores my transgressions, I reckon I can keep her little secret. It's this venison I'm concerned about at the moment."

Still ashen-faced and staring at Longarm, Zeena whispered quickly, "Tell him what he had in mind is fine."

Grinning, Longarm turned to the door. "What you had in mind is fine, Sandy."

"Thank you, sir. Good night, ma'am." With a self-satisfied chuckle, Sandy shuffled off down the hall.

When his footsteps had drifted away from the door, Longarm looked back down at Zeena. She was fingering her lower lip pensively and staring back at him, lamplight flashing in her eyes, glistening on her plump red lip. Her full breasts and pink nipples peeked out from between her elbows.

Suddenly, she rose, placed her hands on both sides of Longarm's face, and kissed him hungrily. Keeping her lips glued to his, she reached down and lightly pumped his shaft with both hands.

When he was hard once more, she pulled away, turned around, shook her hair down her back, and raised her round, creamy ass in the air. She grasped the headboard's brass spools with both hands.

"Okay," she said, giving her head another marelike shake and spreading her knees. "Let's resume your recovery, Marshal Long!"

Watch for

**LONGARM AND THE
WOLF WOMEN**

the 341ST novel in the exciting LONGARM
series from Jove

Coming in April!

GIANT-SIZED ADVENTURE FROM AVENGING ANGEL LONGARM.

LONGARM AND THE OUTLAW EMPRESS
0-515-14235-2

WHEN DEPUTY U.S. MARSHAL CUSTIS LONG STOPS
A STAGECOACH ROBBERY, HE TRACKS THE BANDITS
TO A TOWN CALLED ZAMORA. A HAVEN FOR
THE LAWLESS, IT'S RULED BY ONE OF THE MOST
POWERFUL, BRILLIANT, AND BEAUTIFUL WOMEN
IN THE WEST...A WOMAN WHOM LONGARM WILL
HAVE TO FACE, UP CLOSE AND PERSONAL.

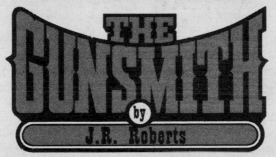